# Long Ride to Purgatory

Shooting the owner of a general store in Cody, Wyoming, was to have dire repercussions for Texas Red Meacher and his gang. As Luther Pickett watches his father die he swears to bring the killers to justice and, with his best friend Skip Jenner, sets out to track the gang down.

However, Red Meacher frames Luther and Skip for a bank robbery and they are both thrown in jail.

The kindness of a wealthy ranch owner for whom the pair have been working sees Luther set free, but Skip must remain in jail until their innocence is proven.

Free at last, Luther has one last chance to find the gang before they escape beyond the frontier of No Man's Land. With justice for his father as well as his own innocence hanging on the line, Luther spurs his horse on. But Luther's world is turned on its head by Red Meacher's own desire for vengeance, before the final confrontation outside the town of Purgatory.

*By the same author*

Dead Man Walking
Two for Texas
Divided Loyalties
Return of the Gunfighter
Dynamite Daze
Apache Rifles
Duel at Del Norte
Outlaw Queen
When Lightning Strikes
Praise Be to Silver
A Necktie for Gifford
Navajo Sunrise
Shotgun Charade
Blackjacks of Nevada
Derby John's Alibi

*Writing as Dale Graham*

High Plains Vendetta
Dance with the Devil
Nugget!
Montezuma's Legacy
Death Rides Alone
Gambler's Dawn
Vengeance at Bittersweet
Justice for Crockett
Bluecoat Renegade
Gunsmoke over New Mexico
Montaine's Revenge
Black Gold
Backshooter
Bitter Trail
The Reckless Gun
Snake Eyes

# Long Ride to Purgatory

Ethan Flagg

ROBERT HALE · LONDON

First published in Great Britain 2015

ISBN 978-0-7198-1561-4

Robert Hale Limited
Clerkenwell House
Clerkenwell Green
London EC1R 0HT

www.halebooks.com



Typeset by
Derek Doyle & Associates, Shaw Heath
Printed and bound in Great Britain by
CPI Antony Rowe, Chippenham and Eastbourne

# CHAPTER ONE

# BLACK DAY FOR CODY

The line of five dust-caked riders was spread out atop a rocky shelf. Below them, standing alone in the middle of a grassy plain was a huddle of buildings. The town of Cody in Wyoming territory was unwittingly receiving their close attention.

In the middle of the group, Texas Red Meacher leaned forward in the saddle. A thick beard the colour of a setting sun concealed a mean slash of a mouth. He pushed back his high crowned sombrero and looked at the town good and hard.

Hooded eyes were keenly surveying the clapboard structures that lined the main street. The penetrating scrutiny revealed that there was no bank. Cody was too small for such an important enterprise. The nearest was at Greybull, some fifty miles to the east. But that was too paltry a target for the ambitions of this outlaw gang leader. He had set his sights on much more lucrative pickings in Casper.

The gang's immediate needs, however, could be adequately serviced here in Cody. And it was the small town's general store that would provide the supplies for which they were so desperately in need. Their saddlebags were all but empty, as were their bellies. The last of their funds had been quickly spent north of the border in Fishtail, Montana. That was after a stagecoach hold-up which had yielded but slim pickings from the five passengers.

Like many owlhooters, the Meacher Gang lived from day to day, spending freely until the source of their ill-gotten gains ran dry. That had been three days before. Since then, they had been forced to live off sticks of beef jerky washed down by weak coffee. Stomachs were rumbling. Nobody even had the wherewithal for a small beer to wash away the trail dust.

Worse for Meacher, however, were the murmurings of discontent becoming evident amongst his associates. The boss was a shrewd desperado who generally managed to keep them all entertained with plenty of booze and loose women. Jobs outside the law had cropped up with surprising regularity over the two years that the gang had been operating.

This was their leanest spell so far.

Only occasionally did a big job come their way. Meacher had been hinting about just such a heist over the last few days to keep his men's spirits up. But there was always somebody ready to challenge his authority.

The last time a rabble-rouser had tried muscling in on Meacher's control of the gang was in Bozeman.

A loud-mouthed galoot called Blanco Vegas had become impatient with Meacher's frequent but small-scale operations. He claimed that the Texas redhead was too old to be running the gang and should step down in favour of a more able leader. Vegas had bragged that he would organize much more profitable ventures than their current leader had undertaken.

Meacher might have been on the wrong side of forty, but he was no slouch when challenged to prove his worth.

Vegas had done all the talking, becoming ever more agitated as he scathingly mocked the older man. Red had listened. His bearded face remained devoid of expression, a blank pretence. After allowing the braggart to jaw himself out, Meacher had carefully removed the unlit cigar stub from between gritted teeth and tossed it aside.

A menacing smile had cracked his hard demeanour.

Then, in a single fluid motion that none of the others could quite believe, he drew both of his Colt revolvers and drilled the loudmouth. Vegas was punched back against the saloon's back wall. A smear of blood trailed in his wake as he slid to the floor with four bullets in his chest, two from each barrel. A silver dollar would have covered the holes, so accurate was the shooting.

That had been three months previous. Nobody had made any show of questioning Meacher's leadership since.

Until now.

Rubin Stagg had joined the gang in the border town of Bridger two weeks before. He was beginning to think he had made a big mistake siding with the redhead.

'The job in Casper better be a good one, Red,' remarked Stagg, throwing a sour look at his leader. 'Another day like this and we'll be chewing on saddle leather.'

Meacher fixed a withering glare on to the speaker. He had not risen to become gang boss by timorous pussy-footing. 'If'n you're nursing a beef, Rube, we can always step down and sort it out here and now with these?' He tapped his pair of matching .44 Colt Frontiers.

The other gang members remained still. In silence they watched and waited. Each of them was well aware of the skill with which Red Meacher handled his nickel-plated hardware. The fate of Blanco Vegas was still talked about from time to time. As was the speed of gunplay by which the rat-faced villain had been despatched.

Stagg immediately sensed that defying their leader's authority, however slight, was fraught with menace. A somewhat nervous look flickered across the faces of the other outlaws. All he received back was a line of smirking faces marked by teeth in varying shades of yellow. Chewing baccy had a lot to answer for out here in the West.

'Just thinking, is all,' Stagg replied, adding with a forced guffaw to ease the crackling tension, 'My belly's rumbling louder than a Cheyenne drum chorus. I could sure demolish a thick prime rib smothered in fried potatoes.'

A couple of the boys smacked their lips, moaning at the thought. Stagg's comments were clearly pervasive among the others.

Meacher accepted the veiled apology with a curt snort. He too was hungry, but mindful of his responsibilities as gang leader.

'Casper'll set us up for a good spell on easy street,' he informed them. 'And that dump' – a loose finger jabbed at the cluster of buildings below – 'will deliver up fresh supplies to tide us over.'

Five pairs of eyes swung back to study the small township.

'That looks like the general store on the end,' remarked a tall, lanky dude pointing to a clapboard building with barrels and tools stacked outside. Jubal Kade then went on to suggest the safest means of robbing the store. 'What do you reckon to us dropping down through that stand of aspen behind? Then we can take them up the ass?'

That received a raucous bout of guffawing which Meacher joined in heartily. He might have been a ruthless leader, but the Texan was always willing to listen to ideas.

He nodded his approval of the proposition.

'A couple o' us could head down all innocent like and walk in the front to draw the attention of the store clerk.'

This postscript to Kade's offering was from Lex Gantry, a tough gunslinger who had been with Meacher from the start. The pair had run with Bloody Bick Shalako's Greybirds. Like the more famous guerrillas led by William Clark Quantrill, the Greybirds had made decisive swoops against Union forces during the War.

Their success had lay in rapidly disappearing to meet up at some pre-arranged rendezvous to discuss their next foray. Plundering and ravaging the countryside, the raiders would create mayhem in their wake. Those were exciting times for young hotheads into which Meacher and Gantry had plunged with gusto.

Following the end of hostilities, life proved decidedly tame in comparison. And it was not long before they began re-enacting their wartime exploits for personal gain. There was also a growing resentment from the defeated forces of the Confederacy against their northern victors. That simmering bitterness had festered in Red Meacher's black heart, often bubbling over into violent showdowns. As a result, he had never allowed any blue bellies to join the gang.

But for now, the tactics nurtured and fruitfully carried out during the grim Civil War were to be re-enacted in Cody, Wyoming.

Meacher chuckled. 'Just like that raid on Springfield back in '64.'

'A classic pincer movement!' echoed Gantry.

'I like it,' concluded Meacher, slapping his thigh with a yip of glee. 'You take Cimarron and Kade to come in from behind. Me and Stagg will make a casual entrance along the main street.'

'You guys must have led one hell of a life.' The Cimarron Kid was too young to have been an active soldier. He sighed, wistfully. 'Sure wish I'd been there!'

'It weren't no Sunday school picnic, Kid,' Meacher chided his young *compadre*. 'Those were tough times. We never knew where our next meal was coming from.'

'Nor if'n we'd see the end of each day,' added Gantry.

It was Rubin Stagg who brought the nostalgic reminiscing back to the task in hand. 'How are we gonna co-ordinate our approaches so they coincide?'

'An owl hoot from me at the back should work,' Kade suggested, having previously displayed his skill with bird impersonations much to the amusement of his sidekicks. 'Hear that and you'll know we're in place and ready to bust in the back door.'

Meacher nodded. The next few minutes were devoted to running over the plan so each man knew his role in the robbery. It was also important that they agreed on the items to be snatched. Only necessities were placed on their shopping list as everything had to be carried in saddle-bags.

Once satisfied, Meacher gestured for Gantry to lead off to the right. He watched as the three men circled around behind a line of crags. Only when they began dropping down towards the tree line behind the town did he nudge his own mount down the slope of the main trail. Stagg followed close behind.

They entered the main street of Cody at the walk. Every effort was made to appear like itinerant drifters just passing through. Texas Red swung his mount over to a vacant hitching rail opposite the general store. A man was sweeping the boardwalk fronting the emporium.

The two watchers dismounted and casually checked their leathers, all the while keeping a weather eye on the premises opposite.

Time passed. Querlies were lit and smoked. But no warning owl hoot was picked up. Meacher was becoming tense; nervous, even. What was keeping Lex and the others? Had they run up against some snags? All manner of questions ripped through his thoughts. Should he and Stagg go in now? Still he hung back. Any trouble and he would have surely heard it.

By this time, the clerk had finished his task and re-entered the store.

Five more minutes slunk by.

Then it came. The haunting refrain he knew so well. A triple hoot that any passer-by would unconsciously assume was the real thing. A sigh of relief issued from between pursed lips. A casual nod to Stagg and they both nonchalantly crossed the street, eyes sweeping the immediate vicinity.

Nobody was paying them any special attention. Grasping the door handle, Meacher pushed open the door and stepped inside. At that moment, Gantry and his bunch emerged from a back room.

Three people were in the store: two customers, and one clerk behind the counter.

Meacher wasted no time in stating his demands.

'This is a hold-up. Raise your hands! Any trouble and you're all dead meat!' The drawn revolvers emphasized that this was no idle threat. 'Check the till, Lex. You other boys grab the goods we need.'

With Meacher and Stagg covering the three innocent

citizens, Gantry and his men coolly went about their allotted tasks. What the gang boss had failed to heed, however, was that the man first seen sweeping the front was not the clerk now standing behind the counter. This guy was a much younger dude.

Meacher discovered his error suddenly when a gun blasted from the head of the stairs connecting with the upper living quarters.

As head of the family business, Sam Pickett had been taking a break from his duties. Age was fast catching up with the old guy. He had run the store in Cody for the last twenty years with the proud boast that not a single day had been lost through illness.

Only during the last few months had he relinquished full control to his son.

Luther Pickett had left home to join the Union cause as soon as he came of age. That had been ten years before, half way through the hostilities in 1863. He had risen from the ranks to become a lieutenant in the 3rd Ohio Regiment of Horse, earning an enviable reputation in the thick of battle.

When the peace was eventually signed at Appomatox in 1865, he had returned home to help his father run the family business. But he was not as dedicated to the mundane rigours of store-keeping as his father, and had pressed that they hire an assistant.

Skip Jenner was tending the store now while Luther enjoyed a well-earned day off. The younger Pickett had been looking forward to escorting his lady friend on a picnic to nearby Horseshoe Lake. They had much to discuss.

Sally Manderson was the latest of a string of girls with whom the handsome ex-soldier had walked out. For some reason, the wearing of his dress uniform – blue trousers with the distinctive yellow stripe, dark blue hat and gloves – appeared to attract female company. Perhaps it was the glamour of being associated with a veteran officer that they found alluring? The exaggerated tales of derring-do had them enthralled as well.

Luther certainly was not complaining.

But Sally was the girl on whom he had lavished most affection. Perhaps, he surmised, this was the woman with whom he was going to walk down the aisle? That was the intention he had mooted to Skip Jenner the previous evening over a game of billiards in the Bighorn Saloon.

Skip had flippantly teased him with a ribald comment. 'You say that about all the gals. So what makes Sally different to the others?'

A mooning cast in his buddy's eyes brought on another bout of hilarity.

'Don't say some dame is finally gonna make an honest man of you?' Skip joshed in good-natured banter.

Luther's face coloured. 'Guess she might be at that,' he blushed, coyly.

Sam Pickett was also well aware of his son's fickle nature when it came to the opposite sex. But he had to admit that Sally was a good catch and Luther had courted her for much longer than was his usual hankering. His son was no longer in the first flush of youth and needed to settle down with a good woman.

Both of them had talked it over for a long time when Luther returned from the saloon.

# CHAPTER TWO

# HARDCAP HORROR

Sam was mulling over the outcome of their heart-to-heart talk when raised voices broke in on his reverie. The harsh tones were emanating from below in the store. They were certainly not those of regular customers. Sam sensed that all was not right. Gingerly, he crept over to the top of the stairs. Shock wrote a clear message across his wrinkled visage on witnessing the onset of a robbery.

Initially stunned, he soon recovered. Caution for his own safety was thrown to the wind. Skip was in danger and needed help.

A robbery had occurred the previous Fall. Two outlaws had held Sam at gunpoint and were in the process of emptying the till when Skip had appeared in the doorway. The assistant was an accomplished handler of firearms and on that occasion had easily outwitted the bungling attempt by the thieves. The two outlaws had stood no chance. They were now occupying a spot in the cemetery outside the town.

Sam saw this as his chance to repay the younger man's brave and resourceful act. In his younger days the old timer had been a town marshal. He had maintained firm order in various camps following the '49 California Gold Rush. Boom towns such as Spanish Flat, Rawhide and Placerville had all experienced the swift justice meted out by Hardcap Sam Pickett.

But that was a long time ago.

Once the initial flurry of excitement had faded and the prospectors had moved on, many of the camps faded into obscurity. A tough town-tamer was no longer required. Hardcap had moved back east of the Sierra Nevada and settled in Cody.

The Navy Colt, however, had been retained, although it had not been fired in anger since those rip-roaring days of yore. That did not prevent the old timer from grabbing up the old firearm now.

He checked to ensure it was loaded before moving quietly out on to the landing. Down below the grating of orders from the gang leader was clearly audible. Sam gave a curt nod. He had been right in his assumption. Sucking in a deep lungful of air, he moved down the stairs cocking and firing the gun from the hip.

But maintaining the prowess of an effective gunslinger requires constant practice – a task the ex-town tamer had neglected. As a result, most of the bullets went wide. Fragments from smashed pots flew every where. Chunks of wood were ripped from the counter close to where Skip Jenner was standing. Bottles of candy exploded in a rainbow of colourful scraps.

Unarmed on this occasion, Skip fumed helplessly, unable to fight back. The customers had hit the floor as soon as the shots rang out. But in such a confined space, even a rusty gun handler could hardly miss.

Stagg clutched at his shoulder. 'I'm hit!' he yelled out, lurching backwards. A pile of brooms were scattered across the plank floor.

Always quick on the uptake, the Cimarron Kid snapped off two shots at the old tin-star. Both found their mark. The Kid had not earned his enviable reputation among the lawless breed for potting clay pipes at the state fair. Sam pitched forward tumbling down the stairs. He was dead before his body finally settled in a heap of bent limbs amidst the debris of his own fusillade.

Luckily for the outlaws, all of the saddle packs had been filled. And Gantry had a wad of greenbacks clutched in his hand.

'Let's ride, boys. We've got what we came for,' Meacher called out, grabbing one of the bags. 'You help Stagg,' he ordered Kade. 'We'll go out the back way. Less chance of being waylaid. Those shots are certain to bring a pile of trouble down on us if'n we hang around here.'

Snatching up the bags, they hustled through to the back of the store and out into the enclosed alley where the horses were tethered. Nobody was about. Any unwelcome reception was likely to be at the front. That was when Red Meacher cottoned to the equally undesirable grasp that two of their horses were also on the main street.

Some of the gang would have to ride double.

'You and Cimarron join up,' he snapped out to Gantry. 'Stagg can ride up front with Jubal.'

The orders were forthright, blunt and decisive. He didn't wait for any dissent that he was the only one not riding double. Such was the ruthless sway that had kept Texas Red Meacher and those who rode with him one step ahead of the law for the last five years. He intended that situation to continue.

Skip's first priority once the bandits had left was for his boss. But following a brief check, it was apparent that Hardcap Sam Pickett had fired his last shot. Skip's head dropped on to his chest as he knelt over the blood-stained corpse. The old man had become the father he never knew. Just like Luther was his surrogate brother.

Then his mind kicked back into action. This killing had to be avenged. Grabbing up the fallen revolver, he dashed out of the back ready to confront the killers.

But only a flurry of dust hanging in the still air indicated which way the outlaws had gone. Of them, however, there was no sign. He hurried back into the store to be greeted by the sheriff, who had just arrived.

Bart Stoneacre was clutching one of the latest cartridge revolvers. Specially developed by Sam Colt's company for law officers, their reliability had quickly earned the meritorious nickname of 'Peacemaker'. Far more serious, however, was that lawless elements had quickly cottoned to the weapon's superiority. Texas Red had acquired a pair from a careless bounty hunter who had tried to arrest him for horse-stealing in Montana.

'I heard the shots!' the sheriff exclaimed. 'What happened?'

Skip succinctly acquainted him with the grim events that had led to Sam Pickett's brutal demise. Stoneacre was dumb-struck. The two lawmen had ridden together for many years before going their separate ways. The marshal had maintained his association with the law, unlike his old friend.

'Why'd the old coot figure he was still the terror of Hangtown?' he mumbled to himself. Tears eked from sorrow-filled eyes. Then he shook off the distraught ache that threatened to overwhelm him. Fretting over what could not be changed was fruitless. What he could do was organize a posse and go after the rats that did this.

'Meet me in the Bighorn in half an hour,' he snapped out. 'There's plenty guys will be keen to join a posse. Old Hardcap was a popular dude.'

'That he was,' concurred Skip, nodding. 'I'll ride out to Horseshoe Lake. . . .'

A quizzical frown creased Stoneacre's brow to interrupt the clerk's outpouring.

'Luther is with Sally Manderson,' Skip said, answering the unspoken query. 'Reckons on popping the question today.' Skip shook his head. His face was ashen. 'I sure ain't gonna relish spoiling his big announcement. But I know he'll want to join the posse.'

The sheriff uttered a sympathetic grunt. But his priority now was the organization of that posse. Every minute wasted accorded the owlhooters more chance to escape, more chance for the trail to go cold.

But the gathering of a suitable bunch of temporary deputies proved harder than expected. Being the middle of the day, there were few men about able and willing to join what might well prove to be a protracted pursuit. Most of the guys that the sheriff would have preferred were working on the ranches.

Of those available in town, many were family men who were reluctant to sign up. Much as they respected Sam Pickett, a sheepish reluctance was expressed about their wives not wanting to see them placed in danger. The sheriff received these somewhat lame excuses with a barely concealed disdain. In the end, Bart Stoneacre only managed to recruit three other men in addition to Luther and Skip.

The younger Pickett was about to plight his troth when Skip arrived at Horseshoe Lake in a flurry of dust. Luther was none too pleased at the untimely interruption. But the grim tidings related by his friend thrust into disarray what was meant to have been a happy event.

The picnic was abandoned. Luther could think of nothing else but joining the posse to hunt down his father's killers. Sally Manderson would have to wait.

In view of the delay, it was four hours after the shooting that the six-man posse finally left Cody. They headed south-east towards Klondike Peak and the scalloped moulding of the Bighorn Mountains. That was the general direction that Skip reckoned they had gone.

Each man carried a revolver, three of which had been supplied from the sheriff's own arsenal. He had also given them all Henry rifles with a supply of ammunition. Supplies were toted for what was expected to be no more than a five-day trek.

The assumption was that they ought to catch up with the outlaws before they hit the Bighorns. Following them into that rocky labyrinth would be like searching for a needle in a haystack. Such gloomy thoughts regarding the outcome of their venture were, however, kept firmly under wraps. Outwardly, the lawman gave every impression that the success of their mission was a mere formality.

Nonetheless, he quickly urged their pace up to a frenetic gallop.

Had Sheriff Stoneacre known that the Meacher Gang was considerably handicapped, he would have been much more optimistic. Being forced to ride double and nurse a wounded man was slowing them down. For each mile covered, Texas Red was becoming ever more tetchy.

'Can't you guys go any faster?' he growled out over his shoulder to the back markers only to find that Jubal Kade and his wounded passenger had fallen well behind the others.

A bleak landscape broken up by weathered crags and gullies did not make their progress any easier. Not especially steep, the undulating nature of the wild terrain was sapping the stamina of both horses and men. Two days had passed since the robbery. The one positive outcome had been the quality of their vittles.

But eating tinned chicken and green beans washed down by five star whiskey had not tempered Red Meacher's ruthless disposition.

He hawked out a lurid curse. Another wasted ten minutes passed hanging around for Kade and the wounded Stagg to catch up.

'You turkeys need to move faster than this,' he admonished Kade. 'That posse will be running us down at this rate.'

'Rube's losing a lot of blood, boss,' the outlaw muttered. 'Go any faster and he's a goner for sure.'

'Then leave 'im,' was the blunt reply. 'He can take his chances like the rest of us.'

Kade was about to protest when Lex Gantry rode up. He had gone ahead to scout out the lie of the land. Hearing the gang leader's brutal reaction to their buddy's ill-fated condition did not sit well.

On the other hand, neither did getting caught by an irate posse who were more than likely to opt for the first directive of a Dead or Alive! policy. The killing of innocent citizens incensed fellow locals more than anything else. Justice at the hands of such pursuers would be swift and terminal.

'There's a relay station up ahead,' he announced in an upbeat tone. 'We can exchange these broken-down nags there. That'll give us each a fresh horse and the chance to outwit any pursuit.'

The good news considerably improved Meacher's sour mood.

'How far?' he asked.

'No more than ten minutes ride,' said Gantry, pointing up the trail. 'It's in a hollow and I counted off five horses in the corral.'

Meacher laughed. It was the first time since the robbery that his leathery features had split. It was a welcome release of tension. 'Looks like we are expected, boys. So let's not disappoint them.' The relief expressed was palpable.

With that cheery comment, he spurred off.

The three blowing horses drew to a halt on the ridge overlooking the shack down below. A well-used highway passed through the broad valley bottom crossing the south fork of the Shoshone River a mile further on. This was the main East-West trail connecting the towns of Jackson and Buffalo. Luckily, there was no stagecoach in sight. But that didn't preclude one appearing at any moment.

Meacher dismounted. Normally he would have ridden his cayuse down the steeply canting narrow zigzag. But in this condition, the mare's legs were more than likely to give way. And the two carrying double were already showing signs of going lame. Another hour and he reckoned they would all have been cast afoot.

The sudden appearance of the small group had not passed unnoticed. 'Looks like we got company, Jim,' Rachel Carmichael remarked to her husband, who was just finishing his lunch. 'And they look a mean bunch of roughnecks,' the woman added.

Hogan Carmichael pushed back his chair and hurried outside, grabbing a-hold of a breech-loading

Sharps rifle from above the fireplace. As the riders drew nearer, he spoke anxiously to his wife.

'They're riding double and one of them is wounded. You're right about these jaspers being trouble. Stay inside while I get rid of them.'

Although these were tough-looking hombres, Carmichael stood his ground. He had fended off marauding Indians, drunken trappers and grizzly bears in the past. There was no reason why he could not handle these varmints. That was what he told his wife. Inside, however, his guts were churning.

The riders halted outside the station. The leader nudged his horse forward forcing Hogan to step back. Red Meacher leaned over the animal's neck. An avaricious eye peered across to the corral.

'Some mighty fine horse flesh over yonder, mister. Could be we can make an exchange. Ours are plumb wore out.' Texas Red's gravelly voice was stating a fact of life. His blunt avowal was no request, but a deliberate act of aggression. Accompanied by a hard and determined regard, it brooked no rebuttal.

But the station manager took up an equally stubborn attitude. He was not giving way to these blustering reprobates. The rifle swung to cover the newcomers.

'They are not mine to trade, mister. The Sheridan Stage Line owns them and it's issued strict rules on how they are to be used.'

'Now ain't that a crying shame, boys?' Meacher's false regret was accompanied by muffled guffaws from the hovering outlaws. 'We sure need those mounts. You see, there's a posse on our tail. And without them those dudes will catch us up.'

While the mocking dialogue was being conducted, Jubal Kade had casually dismounted and moved across to admire the fresh cayuses. On the other side, Lex Gantry was ostensibly filling his water bottle from a bucket. Carmichael shuffled his feet nervously. He only had one set of eyes in his head.

Before he knew what was happening, Gantry had stepped up behind him. The outlaw's gun butt crashed across the back of the manager's head. He went down in a heap. The groaning brought his wife outside.

'Hogan . . . Hogan . . . are you all right?' A cry of anguish issued from the distraught woman's lips as she dashed across to tend her moaning husband.

'He's all right, lady,' scoffed Meacher, coldly pushing the woman away. 'The guy's a tough old buzzard; he'll live. Now rustle up some grub while the boys saddle them fresh mounts. And make it snappy. We ain't got time for hanging around.'

'What about my husband – you can't leave him there!'

Displaying an evident lack of enthusiasm, Meacher relented. 'OK, you have five minutes. But first clean up Rube's shoulder and dress his wound.' His next order was to Cimarron. 'You keep an eye on her, Kid. Make sure the old dame don't pull no fancy tricks. And one more thing, lady.' Rachel Carmichael paused, a cold eye regarding the gang boss. 'When's the next stage due?'

'Don't worry,' the tenacious woman snapped out in her most disdainful nuance. 'There ain't another one until tomorrow noon.'

'No need to hurry with the grub then,' replied Meacher, satisfied. 'So make sure it comes good and hot.'

A half-hour later, the gang were ready to leave.

'Much obliged, lady. That was a sight better than trail chow any day.' Meacher's praise for Rachel Carmichael's culinary skills was genuine. But that didn't stop him and his men ransacking the house for fresh supplies. They also commandeered the station armoury and ammunition. 'No sense in putting ideas into your head while we're riding away, is there?' A sidewinder exhibited more humour than Texas Red's partisan smile.

His wife's tender ministrations had worked wonders for Hogan Carmichael. As the gang were preparing to leave, the station manager lurched over to the door of the cabin and called out, 'The posse will catch you jaspers, and I'll be there at your trial to applaud as the judge sends you all down.'

Meacher's reaction was a mocking guffaw. 'Not a chance, old timer. These fresh horses are our guarantee of immunity.' He despatched a couple of bullets over the old dude's head. Then, with a final halloo the outlaws galloped off in a cloud of dust.

# CHAPTER THREE

# AND THEN THERE WERE TWO

It was not until the following morning that the Cody posse reached the Sheridan Depot. It had been a hard ride. The horses were tired, as were their riders. They were looking forward to a hearty meal prepared by the station manager's wife. Rachael Carmichael was well-known throughout the territory for her varied and tasty menus.

Sheriff Stoneacre knew that they would need to rest up here for a spell. Heads drooping under the intensity of a hot sun, the animals were clearly bushed, all-in. Hopefully, once they had been watered and grained, the respite would have revitalized them sufficiently for the next phase of the pursuit.

Would a couple of hours be enough? Stoneacre was under no illusions. Unless the posse caught up with the gang before they reached Hole-in-the-Wall, he knew they would be stymied.

Just like the gang on the previous day, the posse drew up on the ridge overlooking the station. All seemed calm and tranquil below. There was no visible sign that the gang had wreaked such havoc on their recent visit.

Had the sheriff been more observant he would have noticed that the horses in the corral were in a sight worse condition than his own mounts. At least theirs were still capable of carrying riders down the acclivitous grade.

Plodding up to the relay station, the posse were met by the manager. The bandage swathing his head indicated that things were not as rosy as had first appeared.

'What happened to you, Hogan?' the lawman enquired, solicitously. 'You been arguing with a loco mule?'

'Same thing but on two legs,' snapped Carmichael. His humour had not recovered sufficiently to bandy words with the visitors. 'We had a visit from a group of skunks who wouldn't take "no" for an answer.'

'That must be the same gang we're after,' Skip Jenner added.

'The leader thought it real funny when his buddy slugged me from behind,' snarled the irate manager. 'If'n I ever get my hands. . . .'

'You boys look plumb tuckered out,' interjected Rachel Carmichael. 'Offer the sheriff and his men a drink of your special brew, Hogan. They've come a long way. And I guess you are hungry as well.'

Six pairs of eyes lit up. Just thinking on the mouth-watering recipes likely to be on offer made their stomachs rumble. Hogan Carmichael's injury was pushed aside as the posse hustled into the cabin. Over a scrumptious meal that amply lived up to all their expectations and more, Stoneacre asked how far behind the gang they were.

'They left here late yesterday afternoon,' the manager replied. 'You'll need to ride hell for leather to catch them up.'

'Our nags need at least two hours to rest up. The only chance we have of catching them afore they reach Hole-in-the-Wall is for you to lend us some fresh ones.' The lawman looked hopefully at his host.

But the optimistic regard was met with one of equal regret.

Carmichael's shoulder's lifted in a display of regret. 'They took all my best horses. Ain't got a single decent mount left. Their nags were so done in I've had to shoot two of them.'

'What about those two chestnuts in the back meadow?' suggested his wife, doling out second helpings of apple and cinnamon pie smothered in cream.

Carmichael clapped his hands. 'Gee, I clean forgot about those two!'

'Are they ready to ride?' The muffled query came from Luther Pickett, his mouth full of the delicious dessert.

'Sure are,' preened Carmichael. 'And they're built for speed.'

'Would you be willing to sell them to me and my buddy?' asked the expectant young man. 'I'll pay you the going rate, and you can keep our horses.'

'You seem awful keen to catch these jaspers,' murmured the astute station manager. 'Is this a personal vendetta? It sure would be if'n I was young again.'

'They shot and killed my pa during a robbery of our store in Cody.' The statement was delivered in a flat monotone devoid of emotion. But there were tears in Luther's eyes. His teeth ground with anger. 'I'll catch up with these rats – even it means going all the way to Mexico.'

'You can have the horses, mister,' said the breezy woman. 'And we won't take a dime off'n you. Ain't that right, Hogan?' It was clear that Rachel Carmichael was no meek and mild sort of woman. The penetrating blue of her sparkling eyes challenged her husband to disagree with the blunt proposal.

'Guess you got yourself some horses,' concurred the old dude. 'My life wouldn't be worth a plugged nickel if'n I refused. Not that I had any intentions of so doing. But you better be heading out soon. Those jaspers have a good head start.'

'Are you two are carrying on, then?' muttered the less-than-eager lawman.

Luther and Skip nodded together.

'You reckon that's a good idea?' asked the sheriff. 'With fresh mounts, they'll have disappeared into the Bighorns afore you reach the Divide. Then you'll never find them. And there's only you two against five. Not good odds – not good odds at all!'

But Luther was adamant. 'I ain't letting the killers of my pa escape, Sheriff. We'll trail them to hell and back if necessary.'

'Well, you're free to make your own decisions, boys,' the lawman said, clicking his tongue in dissension. 'But I can't chase all over the territory and beyond if'n I don't figure there'll be a result at the end. Even for old Hardcap. The mayor would have my badge.'

Ten minutes later, Hogan Carmichael returned from the north meadow with the two horses. He had not been exaggerating. These were prime pieces of horse flesh. Luther insisted that the station manager accept some money for the animals.

'We have no way of knowing when, or even if, we'll be heading back this way.'

It was a poignant moment for them all when the two men rode out.

'Good luck, boys!' Carmichael called after their disappearing backs.

'They're sure gonna need it.' The pessimistic comment from Bart Stoneacre was supported by the remaining posse men.

The five members of the Meacher Gang were drawing close to the impenetrable upthrust of cliffs known as the Devil's Grin.

Only one place in the sprawling line of red sandstone offered a way through the mountain fastness. And that was the notorious gap known to lawless brigands throughout the West as Hole-in-the-Wall. It offered a safe haven free from the depredations of tenacious lawmen.

A thin trail snaked up through a fissure – if you could locate it. Once over the lip, it was easy to disappear amidst the numerous valleys on the far side that comprised the Bighorn Range. The gap could easily be protected by a single man with a rifle. As a consequence, no official law officer had ever managed to successfully penetrate this revered hideaway. Some had tried, but had never returned to civilization to crow about their endeavour.

Bart Stoneacre knew of three such star-packers. He had no intention of joining their buzzard-pecked bones in the infamous playground.

Rubin Stagg was rocking in his saddle. The severe jolting occasioned by Meacher's insistence on keeping up a fast pace had restarted the bleeding of his bullet wound.

Kade pushed his mount to the head of the line. 'Rube is lagging behind again. He needs to rest up, boss,' he appealed to the gang leader.

But Texas Red's hard features remained devoid of sympathy. 'We ain't stopping for nobody. That posse could be closer than we think. Anybody who can't keep up will be left behind to take their chances.'

There was no point in arguing with the callous outlaw. Reluctantly, Jubal Kade threw a regretful look back to his buddy, now more than two hundred yards to their rear. His own survival came first; Stagg would have to be abandoned. Thirty minutes later, and the wounded man was no more than a distant speck.

It was lucky for Stagg that his horse had picked up the scent of a nearby chicken farm. The isolated holding lay on the far side of the arroyo along which the gang had been heading. Just as the animal came within sight of the small log cabin, Stagg slid out of the saddle.

A dog barked, alerting the farmer to the fact that he had company. The riderless horse trotted into the fenced yard fronting the twin-roomed abode, scattering a hoard of squawking chickens in its wake. Grabbing hold of the flapping reins, a tall, lanky negro quickly brought the animal under control. His portly wife of Indian extraction pointed to the still form some hundred yards away on the ground.

'What in the name of Hiawatha has happened here?' the negro exclaimed in a deep resonant voice. He had always been known simply as Mudlark. An ex-plantation slave, he had been given the lugubrious name by his owner.

The big man did not expect an answer to his startled query. Nor did he receive one. With the dog at his heels, he hurried off to determine the condition of their macabre guest. The woman waited outside the cabin until her husband returned carrying the slight form of Rubin Stagg in his arms as if he were a newborn calf.

Then she came to life ushering them into the cabin where he was laid out on a spare cot. 'This man badly in need of Shoshone healing if he is to live.' The woman's forthright declaration was followed by instructions for her man to boil some water while she procured the necessary ingredients from her medicine chest.

While the wounded man was still unconscious, Wind That Breathes carefully extracted the bullet. A foul-smelling salve comprising extract of skunk cabbage, dried yarrow seeds and wild mint, was next applied to the ragged wound in Stagg's shoulder. Satisfied with her work, the Shoshone squaw began chanting in a tuneless croak. Pudgy hands waved over the supine body as she swayed back and forth like a cornered rattlesnake. The intention was to drive out evil spirits, thus enabling the concoction to repair the injured body.

Although Stagg remained unconscious for the rest of that day, Wind's tribal ministrations must have worked. Next morning the outlaw's pale eyes flickered open for the first time. The fever had passed, although he was still extremely weak, having lost much blood.

Thankfully, however, he no longer appeared to be past the point of no return.

The squaw fed him chicken broth while her husband waited anxiously for the man to explain the circumstances that had led to his dire situation.

'How did you come to be wounded, mister?' Mudlark tentatively enquired when Stagg signalled he had had sufficient of the nourishing repast. His left shoulder was swaddled in a bandage. Stagg was about to make up some excuse when a stentorian demand cut into the tranquil atmosphere.

'I know you're in there, fella.' The voice belonged to Luther Pickett, and he was in no mood for any chicanery. 'Come out with your hands up!'

The two hunters had spotted the tracks where the lone horse had deviated from the trail. When they had come in sight of the solitary farm, they had paused. Skip had pointed to the horse outside the cabin. The Sheridan brand on its rump proved that it was one stolen by the gang.

'Looks like the injured varmint has been abandoned,' was his blunt comment.

'He must have holed up in that cabin,' added Luther. 'How do you figure we should tackle this?'

A plan was quickly formulated as the two men moved in on the lone cabin.

Stagg's right hand automatically reached for the six-gun resting in its holster beside the cot. Even in his parlous state he knew that if he surrendered, a hefty jail term would be his least reward. More than that, being the only gang member to be caught, he would get all the blame. A neck stretching was likely to follow.

The two benefactors had been good to him, but now it was a question of survival.

Stagg's gun swung to cover them. 'Tell him there's only the two of you here and to come in.' His voice was low yet menacing in its intensity. 'Any funny business and you'll answer to this.' His hand waved the palmed revolver. But in his parlous state, Stagg had forgotten about his horse outside.

Mudlark nervously stumbled to his feet. 'Come along inside, mister,' he called out, a tremulous waver in his reply. 'Ain't nobody here but me and my woman.'

The sound of boots scraping the ground heralded Luther Pickett's imminent arrival. Stagg's gun was aimed at the doorway ready to blast off the minute he appeared. The scuffling ceased outside. For a brief moment silence ensued. Then the door creaked open. But nobody stepped inside. Stagg was primed for that exact moment. His gun spat lead, two bullets ripping chunks from the door where the intruder ought to have been. But nobody appeared.

Wind That Breathes screamed. Mudlark pulled her down on to the dirt floor, shielding the trembling squaw with his body.

Then another gun erupted to the right of where the wounded man was lying. Skip Jenner was leaning in through the window. His bullet did not draw blood but it was well-placed. The Smith & Wesson flew out of Stagg's hand.

'Aaaaarrgh!' he yelled. The desperado had been outwitted. He fell back on to the cot. But at least he was still alive. The accurate shot had smashed the gun-butt, effectively disarming the miscreant but leaving him otherwise intact.

The two men scrambled into the cabin. A pair of grim faces hovered over the quaking outlaw. Killing him would not have achieved anything. Their ultimate aim was to secure information from the wounded man regarding the gang's destination.

'Where are your buddies headed?' rapped Luther. A grasping hand was ready to shake the information out of the sagging frame, if necessary.

There was no need, however. Stagg knew that he was unable to retaliate. He was also aware that Red Meacher had abandoned him to his fate. The wounded bandit understandably felt no sense of loyalty to his old comrades.

Threatening guns poking at him helped to make up his mind.

'Don't shoot!' he burbled. 'I'll talk. Those critters

ain't no friends of mine. Meacher aims to cross the Bighorns. He's heading for Casper. They plan to rob the bank of all the herd money deposited by the cattle outfits following the round-up.'

Luther cast a knowing eye towards his partner.

'So why d'you stop in Cody?' he rasped.

'We needed supplies. Simple as that. There wasn't meant to be any shooting. The old dude should have kept his nose out.'

Stagg's cavalier attitude to his father made Luther see red. He grabbed the wounded man. An arm rose to smash a brutal fist into the sneering face. 'That was my pa you shot down,' he snarled. It was only the quick intervention of his buddy that saved the outlaw from a severe beating.

'Easy there, Luther,' Skip appeased his friend, pulling him away. 'We don't want to sink to the level of this sewer rat by attacking a helpless man, even if he is a lowdown skunk of a killer.'

'Guess not,' replied Luther, backing off. 'I just lost my head for a minute there.'

'It weren't me that killed the old man,' whined Stagg. 'That was the Cimarron Kid's doing.'

Skip's eyes widened. 'I've heard about him. Ain't he the dude that bested Coyote Bill Frayne over in Kaycee last Fall?'

Stagg nodded. 'He's a hothead, to be sure. You guys'll need to be wary of him. A real slippery jasper.'

He went on to apprise the two hunters of how to locate the concealed entrance to the hidden valley by way of Hole-in-the-Wall. It was clear from his outpouring that Rubin Stagg had no compunction about shopping the gang.

'If'n we do manage to bring them back alive, I'll make sure to speak up for you,' Luther promised the wounded man.

His amended attitude in no way excused the outlaw's participation. But Luther knew that without Stagg's co-operation they would have been hard-pressed to run the other varmints to earth. At the same time, he was well aware that the outlaw's disclosure had only come about due to the gang having deserted him.

Stagg appeared to read Luther's thoughts.

'They ought not to have left me. That would never have happened when I ran with the Nevada Blackjacks. Rafe Culpepper knew how to look after his men. That is, 'til he ran up against a firebrand half-breed called Cheyenne Brady.* It was only Jubal Kade who showed any pity. And he left me when Meacher gave the order.'

The man's thin mouth twisted into a snarl of hatred. Now that he had opened up, Rubin Stagg was ready to trill like a canary. 'I know I'm going down for a good spell. But if'n you boys catch up with them, I'll be ready to testify at their trial.'

Stagg then turned to address Mudlark and his wife. 'Much obliged for all your doctoring, ma'am,' mumbled the contrite outlaw. 'I wouldn't have made it without your help.'

* The story of Rafe Culpepper and his clash with Cheyenne Brady is told in *Blackjacks of Nevada* by Ethan Flagg, Robert Hale, Black Horse Western (2014).

The wounded man had divulged all that he could. The pursuers were now ready to continue their quest for vengeance.

'If'n one of you good folks could go for the posse at the Sheridan Relay Station before they leave, somebody can fetch a buggy to take this jasper back to Cody.'

'One more thing before you leave, mister,' croaked Stagg, raising himself on to one elbow. 'How did you find me?'

Luther smiled. 'Your horse led us here. And you were leaking blood like a sieve. Guess you weren't in no fit state to watch your back.'

Stagg responded with a resigned nod of comprehension.

Skip was already outside mounting up. 'Come on, Luther,' he called out. 'There ain't no time to lose if'n we're to catch up with Meacher and his gang.'

# CHAPTER FOUR

# THE BARWISE BRAND

It was a week later when Texas Red led the remaining members of his gang out of the Bighorn Mountains. Deadman's Gap was the final mountain pass after which the terrain angled down into the foothills of the Powder River. Rich grassland enabled large cattle herds to prosper. As height was lost, they encountered small groups of cowboys gathering in the strays that had roamed far from their home pasture during the winter months.

It was round-up time. Older steers would be driven to the markets based in Casper. There they would be sold to buyers from eastern cities such as Chicago. The bank in Casper would be bursting at the seams with cash. And it was this lucrative prospect that Red Meacher intended to exploit.

An avaricious gleam took in the thousands of cattle scattered across the grassy plain below where he and his men were observing the age-old ranching process at work. Round-up was a busy time when men worked from dawn 'til dusk to ensure all cattle were marked with the appropriate brands. These were the marks burnt into the cow's hide to signify ownership. Rannies who could neither read nor write were nevertheless able to name outfits from the brands.

Although exhausting and often dangerous, cowboys enjoyed round-up. It was a time when they could meet up with old pals and make new ones. A conscientious guy could prove his worth at round-up. All his skill and dexterity were needed to do the job effectively. Anyone who showed promise could expect to be taken on permanently. Many cowboys could be seen circling around, cutting out young calves and mavericks ready for branding.

A tally was kept of all those belonging to the numerous different ranches, each with its own distinctive mark. Honesty and accuracy were essential qualities of the man assigned to this important task. These animals were then herded together into a temporary corral.

Representatives from other ranches would drive their animals back to the home range.

One of the most respected of the ranchers in the Powder Valley was Robson Barwise. This grizzled veteran was one of the first 'punchers to stamp out the renowned Goodnight-Loving trail from Texas. Once he reached Wyoming, Barwise had recognized the territory's potential as a cattle-rearing paradise. He had stayed on and amassed his own herd, which was now the biggest in the Powder River country.

He adopted a clever ploy to establish ownership of his own steers by using the two syllables of his name. Brands came in all manner of shapes and depictions, yet few matched the creative imagination of Robson Barwise. And thus the spread came to be known as 'the Bar Ys', its distinctive brand becoming synonymous with enterprise and dogged determination.

It so happened that this was the ranch that Red Meacher found himself surveying from a low knoll one fine morning in May. Because the task of checking all the cattle was so huge, there was always room for new hands to sign up. They were usually employed on a temporary basis until all the work was completed.

This was to Meacher's advantage.

'Here's where we split up, boys,' he said. 'Me and Lex will go into Casper and suss the place out. You two head down there and join up with one of the cattle spreads. They're bound to be short-handed at this time of year.'

'Why us?' rapped a disgruntled Cimarron. 'Round-up is darned tough work.'

Meacher fixed a steely glint on the grumbling Kid. 'Because I say so,' was the blunt response. 'Unless you figure I ain't running this outfit?'

The snarled challenge was received in silence by the brash Kid.

'And if'n that ain't enough, you two have far more experience of working cattle than Lex or me. We're only good at stealing them. Not to mention the fact that four guys hanging around Casper is bound to attract unwelcome attention.'

Kade shrugged. Meacher had a good point. He and the Kid had both worked on cattle spreads. But a dollar a day all found did not appeal to men who railed against hard graft. Rustling the cattle they were meant to be tending, then altering the brands and selling them to the army was a sight easier, and infinitely more profitable.

'Keep your eyes and ears peeled, boys,' Meacher ordered the two new cowhands. 'I need to know when the cattle are going to be sold. That's when the bank will be ready to receive our expert attention.' This comment had all four men guffawing.

Cimarron and Kade then swung down the shallow grade while the other two continued along the mesa rim towards Casper. The two potential cowhands headed straight for a plume of smoke where the branding was taking place.

Barwise senior's son, Jay, was in charge of the task. He was supervising the latest batch of calves brought in by his men. He looked up as the two newcomers approached, and their dust-stained appearance did not impress the young man. More to the point, the low-slung hardware gracing their hips spelled trouble.

Jay laid aside the hot iron with its well-known design and faced the two riders. 'Can I help you fellas?' he asked, squaring his shoulders. The tone was less than cordial. He sensed an aura of shiftiness hanging over them. Jay had met their kind before: any chance to shirk and they took it. 'We're kinda busy at the moment, as you can see.'

'That's maybe where me and my buddy here can help out,' countered Jubal Kade, adopting a more appeasing manner. 'We've come south from Montana hoping to find work down here. Any chance of a job with your outfit?'

Jay pushed his hat back. His tanned face was cloaked in sweat. Branding was a hot task. He looked the two men over. Maybe they were on the level. There was no reason to suppose that they were other than what they claimed – genuine cowpokes looking for work. The territory was full of them.

And there was no denying that he could use the extra help. At this rate, they would still be branding until Doomsday.

'You guys worked on many spreads?' he posed.

'Cimarron here is a sound bronc buster.' Kade slung a thumb his buddy's way. 'Our last jobs were with Henry Challenger's Walking Seven up in the Deer Creek country. That was last Fall. We then took some line cabin work over the winter months with Corby Dukes. He runs the Diamond Slash.'

Jay nodded. He had heard of both spreads. 'Guess you know what needs doing, then,' he said. 'OK, I'll take you on for the usual wage until round-up is finished.'

Kade smiled. The plan was working out just as Texas Red had predicted.

'Much obliged, mister. You won't regret it.' Kade held out a hand. 'The name is Jubal Kade. This is my partner, the Cimarron Kid.'

Jay accepted the proffered hand. 'Stow your gear in the chuck wagon, then go see Cookie about some grub. Soon as you're done, come back here.'

The two outlaws went about their allotted tasks over the next two days. Tentative enquiries were made as to when they expected the round-up to be completed. All the ranches in the area were pushing for an end-of-month deadline. That would be in another two weeks' time.

Whiskers Flannigan, the cook, was the most garrulous of all the hands. Always ready with a story to tell, he knew all the gossip from around the spreads. It proved a deceptively easy task, therefore, for Kade to lead the chatty pot-stirrer round to the forthcoming cattle sale during a break one morning.

'The boss wants to have the herd sold off by the end of next week,' Whiskers iterated, handing round a plate of his home-baked biscuits smothered in rich gravy. 'The new calves will be saved for next season's breeding.' The old cook lowered his voice to effect an air of mystery. 'The word is that if'n we get a push on and finish early, every man will earn himself a bonus.'

Along with the other avid listeners, Kade made suitably appreciative noises. At the same time he winked at his buddy. Cimarron smirked back with a nod of understanding. They were intending to procure a far bigger bonus than the few bucks doled out by Robson Barwise. The food was wolfed down. There was no denying – the old dude sure was a first-rate cook.

The general chatter was interrupted by the staccato order from his son, Jay Barwise.

'All right, you guys,' he called out. 'On your feet. There's still a heap of eager steers just itching for your tender loving care.'

With a clattering of tin mugs and shuffling of feet, the cowhands rose as one to continue with the seemingly endless work. But at least they were now aware that extra dough was in the offing. It proved to be a positive incentive as they set to with added zest while humming various cowboy melodies.

Three days after Kade and Cimarron signed on with the Bar Ys outfit, two other riders appeared on the horizon. Luther Pickett and his buddy sat their mounts at exactly the same place as the Meacher Gang. But they were in a far less upbeat mood. The trek through the Bighorns had been tough. More than one fruitless decision had found them heading up box canyons.

'I can see now why Stoneacre had no relish to tackle this wilderness,' a morose Skip Jenner had commented acidly for the third time.

Luther merely scowled. 'Without the help of that injured galoot, we'd never have made it this far.'

'No wonder so many outlaws seem to just disappear into thin air.'

But eventually they did manage to pick out the correct route thanks to the help given by a wandering trapper. Foxy Johnston had been roaming these mountains for years. He claimed to know all the gangs that made use of Hole-in-the-Wall, including the James Boys, Sam Bass and the Harpers.

The two man-hunters stayed the night with Foxy, who

regaled them with a host of tall stories. But at least they ate well. Foxy was a good cook and knew how to trap the numerous deer, squirrel and rabbit, together with his namesake.

'Just follow your noses south-east until you spot a tall stack called Roughlock Needle,' he instructed them while gnawing on a juicy hunk of venison. 'Keep left of it through Deadman's Gap and you'll soon reach the Powder River country.'

And so it had proved.

'How are we going to locate those jaspers amongst all the cowpokes down there?' Skip posited, indicating the teeming cattle and their minders milling about in the broad river valley. 'Be like searching for four needles in a haystack. They could even be in Casper by now plotting to rob the bank.'

It certainly was a problem.

'All we can do is sign on with one of the spreads to earn some dough,' suggested Luther. 'Then wait for them to have a go at the bank. At least then we'll be able to join up with another posse and be on their tail quick as a flash. And we know that their leader is a redhead with matching beard.'

When the two men rode into one of the camps, they encountered Jay Barwise. On this occasion, the ramrod was more than happy to sign them up. It would bring his crew to full strength. Now they should have no trouble meeting the sales deadline. And these two rannigans looked a sight more congenial than the other two.

'Glad to have you boys with us,' said Jay. 'Come and

meet the rest of the team. You're just in time to sample the chow cooked up by old Whiskers here. Let's hope it ain't burnt to a cinder like yesterday.'

The cook puffed up his narrow shoulders, his grizzled beard wafting in the slack breeze. 'Less of the old, young Jay,' snorted the feisty cook. 'Me and your pa were branding mavericks when you were knee-high to a cricket. He never complains about my vittles. And anyways, it were your fault the food was off. I sounded the bell and you just kept the boys working. So what can you expect?'

Jay laughed along with the other hands. There was no answer to that solid piece of logic. He held up his hands apologetically.

The boss's son was only joshing. In truth, Whiskers was the best cook in the valley. His son-of-a-gun stew sure was some'n else.

'So what's on the menu today, Whiskers?'

'Step over here and you'll soon find out,' shot back the cook, waving a ladle in the air. 'And you're in luck. It's fresh, hot and waiting to jump on to your plate right now. You boys ever tasted Jack Rabbit Pot Roast?'

'Can't wait,' said Skip, holding out his plate.

During the meal, the two newcomers introduced themselves.

'Say, you ain't related to Sam Pickett from Cody, are you?' Jay asked. He immediately sensed from their grim expressions that all was not right with his latest recruits. 'Was it some'n I said?'

It was Skip who provided the answer. 'Sam is Luther's pa – or was. He was shot and killed in a hold-up. We've come south looking for his killers.'

'Sorry to hear about that, boys,' Jay commiserated. 'Sam was well-respected throughout the territory.'

It was lucky for the hunters that two of their quarry were over on the north range gathering in strays at that moment and so didn't hear the startling revelation. Otherwise, things could have taken a far more ominous turn for the two newcomers.

Over the next few days, Luther and Skip established themselves as hard grafters. The other hands respected them for it.

# CHAPTER FIVE

# THE POT BOILS OVER

But there were some who held a certain grudge against one of the new hands.

Half the Barwise crew had sided with the Confederacy during the Civil War. Many were too young to have fought, but all had lost kin in the bloody struggle. The older men who had been called to arms told stories of the bitter rivalry that still existed, even after all these years.

There was no animosity towards the Barwise family, who were northern-bred. A good boss would always outweigh any past niggles. And the war was long gone. Nevertheless, for some it still rankled.

One source of contention was that Luther Pickett still wore his old Union britches. The dark blue pants with their distinctive gold stripe had received numerous sarcastic comments already. Some of the hands figured the new guy was rubbing their noses in the trough by wearing them.

Luther had no idea that he was the unwitting cause of this dissension. Had he known about such a belief, he would have been mortified. The truth was, he had been pole-axed by the traumatic ordeal of facing up to his father's brutal slaying when Skip first informed him at Horseshoe Lake. No thought had been given to changing into his more regular gear.

As yet nobody had challenged the young man openly. So none of these comments had so far reached the ears of the two partners as they went about their daily chores. But things were hotting up. Sooner or later trouble was bound to erupt.

Bull Anders, a tough hardcase who had lost a brother in the War, began by instigating an argument with Luther about the pros and cons of the conflict. No aggressive overtures had been made by the Kentuckian. The offending trousers did not enter into the discussion. But the mood had become a mite prickly. Any talk about the dreadful conflict was apt to engender a fiery discussion that could easily lead to physical confrontation.

Indeed, on both sides, most of those present had lost somebody in the bloodshed. The men were sitting around the camp having their midday meal.

Some of them agreed with Bull's assertion that the southern plantations could not have operated without black slaves to work the cotton fields. Others held the notion that no man should have the right to own another.

The group broke up before any conclusion was reached. One of the hands pointed to a distant speck heading in from the south quarter. Jay Barwise had been delivering some calves to a neighbouring spread. Nobody wanted to be seen as a shirker by the tough ramrod.

Jubal Kade and his buddy had been sitting to one side. Neither man would have recognized Luther Pickett, him being out of town at the time of his pa's murder. And Skip had had his back to these two jaspers during the robbery.

Kade's home farm in Missouri had been burned down by rampaging blue-bellies and his father strung up to a tree for supposedly supplying food to the rebels. A simmering hatred for all-things northern had festered over the years. It had got him into numerous scraps, usually when he was the worse for drink.

Seeing and hearing Luther Pickett apparently flaunting his northern sympathies was the catalyst that finally allowed the pot to boil over. All of Kade's seething hatred was focused on the ex-bluecoat. He had not spotted the imminent arrival of the boss's son. Nor would he have backed off even if he had, him being a northerner. His dander was up. And nothing short of a tangible showdown would satisfy him.

He had about fifteen minutes to re-fight the War before Jay Barwise arrived back.

Luther had just thrown his old army saddle-blanket over the back of a fine grey mottled Appaloosa stallion. Kade saw his opportunity to challenge the Union man.

'Get your stinking blanket off'n that horse, mister!'

The bluff mandate drew the attention of the other cowboys. Luther's sparkling blue eyes briefly turned to study the speaker. Then he just carried on getting the horse ready for work. Kade's hoarse bellow was completely ignored. 'I said leave that horse alone. He's mine,' he repeated in a more aggressive manner.

The snarled directive now saw Luther facing the challenger who came strutting across followed by the Cimarron Kid.

Luther didn't want any trouble. He attempted to quell the guy's bluster with reason. 'The boss told me to cut out a horse I fancied. This Appaloosa was going spare so I figured to borrow him while I'm working here.'

Kade brushed the olive branch aside. 'Well, it so happens that I booked this cayuse yesterday,' he snapped in reply. 'So you go find yourself another one.'

Luther surveyed the gathered cowboys, his gaze settling on the wrangler. Bronco Travis stepped forward, answering Luther's unspoken question. 'Nobody has reserved any mounts, mister. You're lying. That right, Louis?'

Assistant wrangler Louis Ortez nodded. 'Sure is, Bronco,' the young Mexican concurred. Both men stood their ground, silently challenging Kade to deny it.

Mouthing curses, the outlaw was not for backing down. He dragged the blanket off the grey. 'I had me this grey spotted before you turned up and no damn Yankee pisspot is gonna take him.'

All attempts at a peaceful solution having failed, Luther's reaction was blunt and unequivocal. This guy was clearly itching for a set-to. And Luther was no milksop. He would accommodate the troublemaker with gusto.

'Leave that horse alone. You heard what Bronco said. Now shuffle off, buddy,' he rasped, stepping round the rump of the horse to retrieve his blanket.

At that moment Skip Jenner butted in. 'You just want to cause trouble, mister. Why not crawl back under a stone before you get hurt?'

Kade emitted a raucous guffaw. 'Another bluebottle come to fight his yeller pal's battles, eh?'

Skip countered with a correspondingly sharp retort. 'If'n he can't beat a dungheap like you, I'll lick your boots, then do the job myself.'

Kade scoffed. He was an experienced bar room brawler, a burly thug who knew all the tricks of winning fist fights. Not wasting any more time on idle jaw-chomping, he swung the heavy blanket round and hurled it at Luther. As the younger man raised his arms to fend it off, Kade rushed in and buried a hefty left, then a right fist, into Luther's exposed stomach.

'Now, let's see if'n you're as good at scrapping as you are at jawing,' hollered the sneaky assailant.

Luther went down but was soon on his feet, backing off to regain his breath. That was when the Cimarron Kid joined the fracas. His sinewy arms grabbed hold of Luther from behind, holding him in a tight bear hug. A leery smirk cracked Kade's stubble-coated face as he came forward to finish the job with a mighty haymaker.

Standing to one side, Skip quickly recovered from the sudden and iniquitous move. The thought flashed through his mind that these guys had no intention of fighting fairly. Well, two could play that game. He slung himself at Kade from the side, knocking him over.

Bronco Travis had also joined in the affray by sticking a pistol in the Kid's back.

'Let him alone, Cimarron,' snarled the little wrangler. 'We don't cotton to underhanded back street tactics in this outfit. Fight fair or we'll run you both out of the valley on a rail.' A roar of approval came from the rest of the Bar Ys crew. Even Bull Anders could not abide braggarts who fought dirty.

'Now both of you shuck them irons.' The wrangler's forthright order was not to be dodged. Both men unbuckled their rigs.

Reduced to a one-for-one contest, the two protagonists cautiously circled each other. It was Kade who made the first lunge. But Luther was ready and stepped to his right. As the lumbering brute staggered past he shot out a stunning right to his adversary's jaw. The crunch of bone on bone echoed around the camp.

But Kade was a tough jasper and shook it off. The fight continued with both men trading punches. Blood was drawn by each, but slowly Luther's youth and his more agile body began to tell on the heavier man.

Knowing that he was losing the fight, Kade decided to resort to his more usual strategy. He had noticed a chain hanging on a fence. Ducking and diving to give the impression he was in retreat, the outlaw backed off towards the fence. His left hand grasped the chain as Luther stepped forward to finish the contest.

Emitting a howl of triumph, Kade made to swing the

heavy chain in a lethal scything motion. His arm had barely moved when it was pulled up short. A gurgle of bewildered dismay issued from the brigand's gaping maw.

'What in thunder is going on?' he bawled out, swinging round to confront the skunk who had thwarted the ignoble tactic. A raised fist was ready to deliver a stunning blow to the miscreant.

Jay Barwise side-stepped the sweeping wallop and delivered one of his own straight to the outlaw's jutting chin. Another jolting left followed it up, dumping Kade on the ground. The ramrod then stood over the fallen hardcase, surveying him with a jaundiced look of contempt.

'I'm glad you made that sly move, Kade,' Jay drawled. The smile creasing his tanned features, however, held no trace of levity. 'I've been wanting an excuse to get rid of you pair of layabouts. I ought never to have taken you on. Draw your pay and get off'n my land, pronto.'

Kade's ugly mouth twisted in a violent scowl. But he held his tongue. He had learned all he could from this bunch of nannies anyway.

'Come on, Cimarron,' he called to his partner, bending down to retrieve his gun-belt and hat. 'Let's go enjoy ourselves among some more sociable company in town. This outfit ain't worth the steam off'n my shit.' The loser's parting remark was lost amidst the general clamour. 'You ain't heard the last of this, Pickett!'

It was an idle threat dished out in the heat of the moment, but one that was to have lasting repercussions.

The other hands all crowded around the winner of

the contest, slapping him on the back. The cowpuncher ain't been born that don't enjoy a good fracas. Luther had won them over in time-honoured fashion.

Jay allowed the high jinks to continue while Luther's marked face was patched up by Whiskers Flannigan. Then he reminded them of the bonus that could only be earned if the deadline was met. That soon brought the celebrations to an abrupt halt.

Once they had left the Bar Ys camp, Jubal Kade and the Cimarron Kid headed straight for Casper. On the way they cooked up a story as to why they had quit the round-up early. They knew that their sidekicks would be in the saloon. As expected, the first terse comment from Texas Red concerned their early arrival in town.

'The round-up was going better'n expected so some of the boys were paid off.' Kade emitted a false sigh of resignation. 'Guess it was last in, first out.'

Meacher accepted the explanation without objection. His regard had focused on Kade's battle-scarred face. His left eye was black as the ace of spades. A hearty guffaw followed. 'Say, Jubal, where in tarnation did you get that shiner?'

'Man, it sure is lucky you ain't no handsome dude like me,' added a mirthful Lex Gantry. The two men were sitting at a table to the rear of the saloon huddled round a bottle.

'Give me a drink,' demanded Kade, grabbing the bottle. The loud comments were ignored. 'A loco steer kicked me,' he rapped out, giving the Kid a warning look, anxious to avoid any further questioning. 'But never mind that. The herd money should be in the bank by the end of next week at the latest. Have you guys figured out a way to grab it?'

'Keep your voice down!' hissed Meacher, pulling his associate quickly into a seat. Kade's virulent irritation had attracted unwanted attention from other drinkers in the saloon. 'Do you want every critter round here knowing our business?'

'Well? Have you?' snapped Kade in a lowered voice. 'That round-up was damned hard work. This job better be worth all our efforts.' Kade was becoming more irritated. 'Me and Cimarron have been doing all the grafting while you two sit around here taking it easy.'

'Cool it there, Jubal,' the Kid cautioned, noting the sour looks being arrowed at his buddy. 'I'm sure the boss has been busy working out a plan of action. Ain't that so?' The conciliatory remark was aimed at calming the rising storm.

'Sure we have,' replied an optimistic Lex Gantry. 'Tex and me have everything under control. All we need now is the dough to be deposited. So let's all simmer down and have a drink. Then we'll let you in on our plan.' He poured them all a glass of whiskey. 'To a successful job,' he said, raising his glass.

They all clinked glasses to the toast.

'And many more to follow,' added Meacher. 'So this is how we play it.'

He then went on to outline the plan of campaign.

# CHAPTER SIX

# A GHOST FROM THE PAST

Another week was required to complete the round-up. Being the largest spread in the territory, Robson had invited the buyers to the ranch where they had been wined and dined to secure the best price. The flattering tactics had worked.

Robson Barwise and his son then headed for the bank in Casper. Two other hands were acting as escort for the money paid out for the marketed cattle.

As they were walking down the main street, it so happened that Meacher and Gantry were ambling towards them.

The gang boss stiffened. A look of uncertainty clouded his rubicund features. Gantry picked up on his partner's sudden display of uneasiness.

'Some'n bothering you, Red?' he quizzed. 'Look like

you've seen a ghost.'

When the two unwitting ranchers had passed by, Meacher turned and gave the younger man a probing shakedown. He knew that guy from some place. But where?

Gantry repeated his question. Something was bugging Red Meacher, that was for durned sure.

'I've come across that younger dude before some place,' he muttered, racking his brains. 'Just can't figure out where.' He continued avidly studying the profile of Jay Barwise as he headed down to the bank with his father.

Then a bell sounded inside his head, a clarion call that suddenly made everything crystal clear. And it was not an edifying recollection, not by a long chalk. Jay's distinctive limp had turned on the light of dawning. He slammed a bunched fist into the palm of his hand. Sergeant Barwise! Damn his blasted eyes!

'That's the lowdown rat who gave me those stripes across my back,' he snarled.

The hate-filled utterance rumbled in his throat. The knuckles of his clenched fist went pale. He paused to regain his breath following the momentous revelation.

'What happened?' asked Gantry in a tentative voice.

The rough scars had been revealed when Meacher had taken one of his rare baths. But nobody had previously summoned up the nerve to enquire as to their origin. This was the first time that Private Red Meacher, ex-Greybird and one-time thorn in the Union's ass, had raised the issue.

'It was after the last raid undertaken by the

Greybirds. Bloody Bick Shalako wanted to leave his mark before Lee signed the surrender at Appomatox.' Meacher shook his head as he re-lived the dismal events. 'It was a total disaster. Shalako was killed along with most of the troop. The survivors, including me, were thrown into a stinking POW stockade. And that skunk' – an angry finger pointed at the rancher's back – 'was the bastard in charge.'

'What did you do to warrant a flogging?' asked a mesmerized Lex Gantry.

Meacher huffed. 'One night we tried to escape. It was a futile effort, doomed from the start, and we were soon overpowered. During the scuffle, I knifed one of the guards. So happened, it was Barwise's brother. He was only a kid who found himself in the wrong place at the wrong time. The court martial was all set to hang me. Then I got a reprieve, six months in the Hole seeing as the War had ended. But not before Barwise decided to add his own unofficial punishment.'

A red mist of unadulterated loathing had gripped Meacher's innards. He started towards the limping figure ahead. Gantry could see what was about to happen. He quickly stepped in front of his buddy, dragging him into a nearby deserted alley.

'Pull yourself together, man!' he urged, gripping the gang leader's arms firmly. 'Pull a stunt like that and all our plans will be shot to pieces. When the job's done and we're in the clear, you can always come back and settle with Barwise on your own terms. Confront him now and we all lose out.'

The logic of Gantry's reasoning appeared to filter

through into the distraught mind of the outlaw boss. His tight shoulders relaxed, the racing heart beat slackened.

'Guess it all came back to haunt me,' he muttered, shrugging off his partner's grip. 'But you're right. The job comes first; Barwise can wait.' He walked back out on to the main street. A malevolent eye focused on the rancher's broad back.

The lob-sided gait had not affected Jay's ability in the ranching business. Most of his time was spent in the saddle. The limp was the result of a sniper's bullet. As a result, he had been put in charge of the prison stockade where Meacher was imprisoned until such time as the captives could be safely released.

Meacher spat into the dust as the two men entered the bank and disappeared. 'But make no mistake, mister. I'll be back. And you'll be dead as a losing poker hand.'

When Robson Barwise and his son returned to the ranch, the temporary hands were paid off. Luther was drawing his money plus a good bonus when Jay nodded to where Skip Jenner was otherwise engaged over by the barn.

'Looks like my sister has taken a shine to your buddy,' he remarked, trying to conceal a wry smile. 'He sure must have some'n. Kitty don't normally cotton to the hired help.'

'The two of us are pulling out soon to continue the search for Pa's killers,' replied Luther, pocketing the folded bills. 'So she's gonna be a mite disappointed.'

Jay fixed him with his most persuasive regard. 'You boys have worked hard for the Bar Ys. And not only that, the regular hands respect you. Sure I can't convince you both to stay on?'

'Much obliged for the offer, boss.' Luther was genuinely impressed by the ramrod's praise, but he knew where his priorities lay. 'Maybe Skip will want to come back this way once our quest is over. But I'll be heading back to Cody where I have a proposal of my own to make.'

Jay gave the remark a puzzled frown but didn't pursue its cause.

'Well, the offer's on the table anytime you boys decide to accept.'

Luther had to do a heap of persuading to induce his younger partner to continue with their quest. Not that Skip had lost the hunger for revenge. He had momentarily had his head turned by a pretty face. Kitty was the first girl for whom he had really fallen.

Their final evening on the ranch passed in a something of dreamy haze. The two star-struck sweethearts had taken a walk down to the banks of the river. When Skip reluctantly informed her that he was honour-bound by his commitment to avenge his partner's loss, she didn't demur. The code of esteem to family obligation was a powerful force in the American West. Any self-respecting girl would have expected nothing less from a potential suitor.

'Of course you must go, Skip!' she stressed, looking him full in the eye. 'Knowing you possess such a high regard for your friend's kin makes me admire you all the more.' Skip was glad that the darkening sky concealed his embarrassment. But in truth he felt ten feet tall. 'I want you to have this,' she said, unhooking a small chain with a gold locket attached. 'It contains a lock of my hair.'

Skip knew that such a gift was truly a pledge that she would still be here when he returned. He could only trust that she would honour that commitment from someone she had only known for a couple of weeks. He was little more than a stranger.

They kissed under the twinkling canopy of stars. It was a magical moment that neither wanted to end. Skip was almost tempted to pack in the search for Sam Pickett's killers. His heart was overruling his head. Staring into Kitty's large pools of deepest mahogany, he almost blurted out his intention.

Common sense, however, prevailed. To do so would have soured their blooming affair before it had even begun. Duty called. Slowly, hand in hand, they walked back to the ranch house. Neither knew when they would next meet.

# CHAPTER SEVEN

# HOODWINKED

Luther and his partner left the Bar Ys ranch a couple of days later. The last Skip saw of his beloved Kitty was a pale face at the upstairs window, a hand raised in farewell. It was a sad moment for the young man. But with Luther's prompting, he soon became immersed in their plan to foil the outlaws.

Arriving in Casper, they took a room at the National Hotel, knowing that the money from the cattle sales was now safely in the bank vault. The expected robbery would, therefore, be imminent. The window on the upper floor of the hotel enabled them to maintain a close watch on the premises of the Casper Savings and Loan.

Skip was lying on the bed, arms behind his head. But he was displaying signs of nervousness. His left eye was twitching. Luther could read the signs.

'Some'n bothering you?' he enquired. The truth was

that the younger man was beginning to worry that they were taking on more than they could handle. He voiced his concerns with some trepidation.

'Don't you think we ought to let the law in on what we know?' he asked, gingerly. 'Two guys up against a gang of hardened outlaws ain't gonna be no Sunday picnic.'

'I've been thinking that way as well,' his buddy concurred. 'But then I figured the sheriff would place armed men on every corner waiting to thwart the skunks. That would be sure to scare the gang off.' He shook his head. 'Better to play it like we said. Wait for them to pull the job. Then join the posse and track them down.'

Skip nodded. As usual his buddy had all the answers. 'Guess you're right, Luther.'

'I sure am, buddy. This way we don't lose track of the rats,' he stressed. 'Remember we don't know what they look like.'

It was true. The two men could not have recognized the gang even had they passed them in the street. Meacher had ensured anonymity by having his men wear full face masks. Luther berated himself for not getting Rubin Stagg to describe the gang. Only by allowing the robbery to take place could they now follow to ensure the culprits were dealt with. Howsoever that might be.

Continuing to peer out of the window, Luther suddenly stiffened.

'Hey, buddy! Take a look at this.'

Skip lifted himself off the bed and hurried across to

join his partner by the window. 'Now, what do you suppose Kade and his buddy are up to?'

The pair of disgraced rannigans were having an earnest conversation with a couple of other dudes outside the Medicine Bow Saloon.

'They seem mighty friendly. Almost as if they know each other,' remarked Skip. 'You don't think those two jaspers could be part of the gang, do you?'

'Now I come to think on it, you could be right,' agreed Luther. 'They arrived in the valley just before us. And they weren't regular cowhands, that's for sure.'

'Could be they are getting ready to carry out the robbery,' Skip shot back, buckling on his gun-belt. Now that some action was about to take place, he felt tense but excited. 'I'll go over to the livery stable and get our horses ready.'

Luther nodded as he continued with his monitoring.

Meanwhile, the gang had broken up. Jubal Kade had gone over to the stable to make sure the gang's horses were also ready for a quick getaway following the robbery. Gantry was the only member of the gang who was assigned to enter the bank. Now inside the building, it was his job to check on any last-minute hitches that could frustrate their plans. He read some advertising literature, then innocently began filling out a form, awaiting the arrival of Texas Red and the Kid.

After readying the horses, Kade had his gun out and was hiding behind the door of the stable. His attention was focused on the bank further up the street. A shuffling behind saw the outlaw spinning on his heel. It was the ostler, who had just risen from his siesta.

'Something I can do for you. . . ?'

The liveryman never managed to finish the sentence. His face paled when he saw Kade's raised gun. 'You ought to have stayed in bed, fella. This is a dangerous time to be wandering about.' Without another word, the outlaw stepped forward and slugged the guy over the head with his gun. He went down like a sack of potatoes.

But Kade was given no time to drag the ostler out of sight. The next instant Skip Jenner appeared in the open doorway. The gloomy interior of the stable prevented him spotting the outlaw's cowardly assault. This gave Kade enough time to conceal himself in one of the stalls.

'You in here, Mr. Soames?' Skip called out, peering around. The moment his eyes became accustomed to the gloom, he saw the bludgeoned liveryman on the ground. Hurrying across, he fell to his knees. 'What happened to. . . ? Aaaarrrgh!'

That was when his own lights went out courtesy of Jubal Kade's revolver. A few minutes later Red Meacher appeared along with the Cimarron Kid to make a final check that everything was ready for the getaway.

'Who's this guy?' he asked.

'One of those cowpokes from the round-up come sniffing around for some reason,' Kade growled, giving Skip's prone body a vicious kick. 'I wonder where his buddy can be?'

'Get him out of sight quick,' urged Meacher. 'We need to be at the bank, pronto. Lex will be feeling lonesome.'

'Someone else is coming,' warned the Kid. 'And guess who it is?'

Kade peeped round the door, a snarl issuing from between clenched teeth. 'That bastard, Pickett. He must be coming to find this dude. Well, I'll soon deal with him.' He signalled for the others to hide.

'Are the horses ready, Skip?' Luther called out, stepping inside the stable. He was given no chance to find out, receiving the same brutish welcome as his partner.

Kade chuckled. He was thoroughly enjoying himself. This was like knocking cans off a shelf in a fairground booth. He dragged the inert body into the stall to join the others when Meacher stopped him. An idea had struck the gang boss that would gainfully shift the blame for the forthcoming robbery on to this pair of dupes.

'Change britches with this jasper.' The snappy order was aimed at Jubal Kade. 'Even with us wearing masks, those Union army pants will be a dead giveaway as to who the culprits are.'

Kade was a mite slow in picking up on Meacher's brainwave as the boss slammed the distinctive cavalry hat on to the outlaw's head.

'Hurry up, darn it!' he rasped out. 'We ain't got time to lose. Cimarron, you help me tie and gag these critters up good and tight so's they can't escape.'

Minutes later and the three outlaws were hustling behind the buildings fronting the main street to emerge close to the bank. Casually, they sidled up to the front door. A quick look around to ensure they were not being eyeballed, then they slipped inside, pulling bandana masks up over their faces.

'Nobody make a move, folks, and you won't get hurt.' Meacher's terse order was backed up by the pair of wagging Colt Frontiers. 'This is a hold-up.' He threw a couple of flour sacks over the counter to the teller. 'Fill these up with bills only. No loose coins. We're travelling light.'

Meacher smiled beneath the mask when he noticed one of the customers shifting his gaze from Kade's legwear up to his hat. Take a good look, mister, he muttered to himself, and remember what you see.

Gantry had been talking to one of the tellers, ostensibly about opening an account when his sidekicks burst in through the door. That was his signal to fix his own mask in place. Nobody had given his unobtrusive presence a second thought. The teller was momentarily stunned. But then he decided to make a name for himself by reaching down below the counter for a hidden gun.

'Not so fast, mister,' Gantry snarled, 'I'll take that.' His own palmed gun encouraged the startled teller to obey. He stuffed the small Colt Lightning into his belt. 'Glad you boys could make it.' The guffaw was a mite nervous as he joined his buddies. 'I was getting anxious.'

Meacher ignored the remark. He was more interested in getting the job done without any trouble. 'Hurry it up with that dough,' he barked at the tellers. 'We ain't got all day.' The bags were filled in double quick time under the watchful eye of the brusque redheaded Texan.

Less than five minutes after entering the bank, the gang had secured as much dough as they could carry. Uttering a final threat of retribution should they be followed, Red Meacher led them through the manager's office and out the back way. Nobody was around as they hustled back down to the livery stable. Once inside, Kade quickly exchanged trousers with the stirring form of Luther Pickett. Painful groans issued from the stunned man.

Meanwhile, the bank manager had raised the alarm as soon as the gang had scarpered. The sheriff was not slow in taking up the chase. Shots rang out as someone spotted the robbers inside the stable. But Gantry and Cimarron were ready for them. A hail of gunfire held off the pursuers while the money was secured on to their horses and the two innocent mugs untied.

'OK, mount up, boys,' Meacher called out, snapping off two more shots at the irate citizens of Cody. 'We're leaving through the back door.'

Before leaping into the saddle, he stuffed some of the bills into the pockets of Luther and Skip.

The gang then disappeared in a thunder of pounding hoofs leaving the two suckers crawling around on the floor. Rubbing sore heads and unsure what had happened, the two men were stumbling around the stable when the sheriff and half a dozen men rushed in.

'That's one of them, sheriff,' shouted one of the pursuers. It was the guy from the bank. 'I recognize those army duds.'

Another man hauled Skip roughly to his feet. 'This critter must be another member of the gang.'

'And look what they've done to poor old Soames,' exclaimed another man, helping the moaning ostler to his feet.

This discovery further incensed the crowd who treated the two saps none too gently. And when the stash of hidden bills was discovered, the mood hotted up to such a high pitch that Sheriff Brace Lincoln was hard-pressed to prevent the suspects being strung up there and then. He pushed the crowd back.

'These men will get a fair trial like any other law-breakers,' he shouted, brandishing his shotgun. 'There will be no vigilante law in Casper while I'm in charge.'

The solid admonishment soon calmed the bubbling ire. Lincoln was a well-respected officer of the law. Leading the growing throng, he marched the sorry pair of innocent dupes up the street.

'You've got this all wrong, sheriff,' Luther protested. 'We were slugged in the stable. It's all a big mistake.'

'Don't give us that hogwash, you thieving rat. I saw you in the bank. Nobody else around here wears Union britches and an officer's hat,' growled Clu Sublette, slinging a surprise fist at Luther. The blow almost knocked him off his feet. Only the press of bodies kept him upright. The fact that his pants had been swapped over did not even register in his bemused state.

'What's happened here?' asked a bystander as the gathering processed up the street.

'The bank's been robbed,' replied Sublette. 'But we caught two of the thieves. The posse'll catch the others.'

Before Luther and Skip could gather their thoughts,

they had reached the jail and been unceremoniously tossed into a cell. Their heads throbbed. The latrine bucket in the corner stunk to high Heaven. And they had been well and truly suckered.

The gang had got away and ensured a head-start by pulling that sly trick. Skip didn't voice his opinion that they should indeed have let the law handle this from the start. Not only had their plans ignominiously fallen apart, but they were now judged to be the prime culprits in a major crime.

The dire situation in which they now found themselves could scarcely get any worse.

# CHAPTER EIGHT

# A PRESENT FROM TEXAS RED

It was the following day before Robson Barwise and his son heard about the robbery. A more startling discovery was that Luther Pickett and his buddy were the principal suspects.

Jay had come to like the two men and hold them in high regard. He would never otherwise have offered them permanent jobs on the ranch. He couldn't believe that either man was involved in a bank robbery. It didn't make any sense.

The two men were mounted up and all set to leave the ranch when Kitty Barwise stopped them.

'Where are you two buzzards off to this early?' she asked.

'We have some urgent business in Casper,' Jay said, not wishing at this stage to alarm his sister as to the correct reason.

'What can be so urgent that you miss out on breakfast?' The girl frowned at her brother. 'That sure ain't like you, Jay.'

Robson gave his son a perturbed look of apprehension. The brief flicker of concern was not lost on the girl. Her freckled face blanched. Something was wrong here. She knew her kin too well for them to hide what was obviously bad news.

'Better tell me the truth,' she threw back at them. 'I know something's up.'

Her father sighed. 'Best tell her, boy. Guess she deserves to know the truth.'

Jay sucked in a deep breath. 'Skip and his partner have been arrested for robbing the bank. Joe Flood, the new blacksmith, just arrived from town and gave us the bad news.'

Kitty's mouth dropped open. The blood drained from her face. She was totally stunned by the discomfiting revelation. 'It can't be true!' she cried out. 'They wouldn't pull a stunt like that. I just know it.'

'We don't think so, either,' said her father. 'That's why we're headed into town right now.'

The girl's face had set firmly into a dogged resolve that her father knew so well. 'I'm coming with you.' Her blunt announcement was unequivocal. 'I know you didn't want to worry me, but I have to be there to support Skip. I . . . I . . . love him.' Tears welled up from her brown eyes. 'We've only known each other a short time, but he's the one for me, I just know it.'

Robson shrugged his shoulders. There would be no

shifting his daughter on this issue. He gestured for his son to dismount. 'We'll have a quick bite to eat while you go over to the barn and saddle up,' he said to his daughter.

The ride to Casper would normally have taken around two hours. The Barwise trio did the journey in under one hour. Their horses were lathered up and blowing hard when the three riders galloped up the main street and hauled up outside the jail. They wasted no words of explanation in responding to the curious probing of onlookers. Inside the jail, Robson took charge.

'Is it true that you have arrested two of my old hands for robbing the bank?' he demanded of the deputy left in charge.

'Sure is. They were identified by a witness at the bank and were even caught with some of the money in their possession,' replied Ben Parker. 'Unfortunately, the rest of the gang escaped. You boys are too late if'n you've come to join the posse. Sheriff Lincoln left yesterday.'

The old guy had been sheriff of Casper before he retired two years before when Brace Lincoln took over. But he still took his deputy's job seriously.

'Can we see the prisoners?' Kitty pleaded. 'I'm sure it's all a big mistake. These men are innocent. They must have been framed.'

'That ain't for me to say, miss,' the deputy replied. 'They'll be tried in a court of law.' The old guy was apologetic. But he knew where his duty lay. 'I'll need your guns before I let you into the cell block.'

After handing over their hardware, the three visitors

spent the next twenty minutes with the prisoners. Luther and Skip each stressed that they had played no part in the robbery and had been set up by the bandits. In turn, both men described their own version of the events that had landed them in such dire circumstances.

It was the army duds that appeared to have caused the most controversy.

'I can only think that one of the skunks swapped trousers with me for the robbery,' Luther iterated, with a shake of the head. Large lumps the size of eggs confirmed that the two men had been pistol-whipped. The townsfolk had brushed the assaults off as no proof of innocence, 'But you have to believe that we had nothing to do with the hold-up,' Luther repeated once again with vigour. 'We're a right pair of greenhorns to have been suckered in this way.'

'Don't worry, boys,' Robson tried to reassure the pair. 'We know you're telling the truth. We just have to convince old Ben of that.'

After returning to the main office, the ranch owner attempted to convince the old lawman that his prisoners were innocent of all the charges. But Ben Parker displayed a stubborn streak that had seen him through many confrontations in the past. Here was the man who had single-handedly tamed Laramie during its rip-roaring days. No amount of persuasion was going to sway his view that the law must take its course.

A fresh tack was called for.

'We go back aways, don't we Ben?' said Rob Barwise, thoughtfully, stroking his bearded chin.

'Sure do,' agreed the old timer.

'And have I ever played you false?'

The remark was received with a puzzled frown. 'Guess not,' came back the tentative reply.

'And you trust me, don't you?'

'Ain't another fella in the whole territory I'd rather have at my back when the chips are down,' Parker acknowledged with obvious sincerity.

Barwise paused before making his final play.

'So if'n I were to ask you to release these guys because I know they are innocent, you'd know that I wasn't lying?'

The deputy had been placed in an awkward position. 'Gee, Rob, I want to help you,' he prevaricated, the thick grey mustache twitching. Unwittingly, he had been manoeuvred into an awkward position. Yet still he doggedly refused to be persuaded. 'But I can't just let them go free. The sheriff would have my guts for garters.'

The shrewd rancher had known this would be the reply. His response had been worked out beforehand. 'What if you were only to release one of them into my personal custody and keep the other prisoner here in the jail. That's fair, ain't it?'

After some more horse-trading to make the old jasper feel like he was not being hoodwinked, a deal was struck.

It was decided, mainly for Kitty's sake, that Luther would be released. He and Jay would then go and join up with the posse. Skip would be held as a kind of hostage; a safeguard to appease the deputy's conscience.

Nevertheless, Ben Parker was still nervous about allowing a prisoner to go free without official authorization. Robson assured him that as the owner of the biggest cattle spread in the Powder River country, he had as much to lose, if not more, should things go awry. That seemed to appease the old guy.

A further guarantee was provided in a letter explaining the circumstances of the bizarre arrangement, which totally exonerated the old lawdog.

After dropping Kitty off back at the ranch, Jay and Luther collected enough basic provisions for what might well prove to be a protracted journey. They then left in the direction the posse had taken, according to Deputy Parker.

Robson had wanted to accompany them. A diplomatic appeal to age and domestic responsibilities from Jay failed to persuade the rancher that chasing desperate criminals across the country was best left to younger men. Only the gentle coaxing from his daughter encouraged the spirited rancher to finally succumb.

Father and daughter waved the two men off, not knowing what the outcome of their dangerous undertaking would be.

Because they were a day behind the posse, Jay suggested they catch up by taking a little known Indian trail. The hazardous route pursued a tortuous line through the Granite Mountains by way of a pass known as Castle Gate. It made use of a narrow ledge high above the thrashing ferment of the Sweetwater River in a steep-sided gorge.

Some of the route had collapsed, forcing the two

men to walk their horses along a narrow shelf no more than a yard wide. It was a heart-stopping experience that left them breathless and shaking with nervous tension when they finally made the far side.

'Guess I can understand now why this trail was abandoned by the Arapahoes some time back,' Jay gasped out as he cast a disbelieving look along the sinuous rim they had just negotiated. Luther saw no reason to disagree.

A stop for some much-needed hot coffee was called to steady their fraught nerves. But at least the short cut had achieved its objective.

Shadowy fingers of late afternoon were creeping across the landscape when the two riders saw a plume of smoke rising above a cluster of cottonwoods up ahead. Approaching the camp with due caution, they recognized it as that of the posse. Although a perilous undertaking, the short cut by way of Castle Gate had saved them a full day.

'Hallo, the camp!' Jay called out so as not to alarm the occupants. 'Two riders coming in.' Arriving unannounced at any time of day would likely have earned them a hot-leaded reception.

The sheriff was surprised to see that one of their visitors was none other than Jay Barwise. He didn't immediately recognize his sidekick, whose features were bathed in shadow.

'Who's your friend?' he asked.

Before Jay could reply, a man stepped forward brandishing his pistol. He was giving the second man a furtive once over. Then his eyes widened in shock. 'Hey,

Sheriff, that's the critter I recognized from the bank job. And he's still wearing those army britches.'

Lincoln stiffened. A gun appeared in his hand. 'You're right, Clu. He's meant to be locked up in my jail.' The lawman was less than pleased to see that one of the alleged robbers was clearly on friendly terms with the son of the most respected rancher in the territory. His following demand was cagey and laced with suspicion. 'What you doing with this dude, Jay?' exclaimed the bemused lawman. 'There better be a good explanation for this.'

The pointing gun along with those of his four deputies ensured that the two men kept their hands well clear of their holstered irons.

Jay quickly and concisely apprised the sheriff of his father's handling of the situation. Brace Lincoln listened without interruption. His face remained an inscrutable mask throughout the heartfelt justification for the action taken. Only when it became clear that the other suspect was still being held in jail did his stoical demeanour soften.

'If'n you weren't the son of Robson Barwise, I'd arrest you here and now as an accomplice.' The veiled threat was half-heartedly accompanied by a wry smirk. Even so, Sheriff Lincoln was still miffed that his old deputy had been talked into releasing a prisoner. That was not the way he conducted the law.

Jay backed up the old timer's decision by countering with a lucid observation. 'We sure wouldn't have ridden in here unburdening ourselves to you if'n we were in cahoots with the robbers, would we?'

Lincoln gave the remark a sagacious nod. 'Guess you wouldn't at that,' he concurred. 'OK, boys, get yourselves some grub. There's grain for your horses in the nosebags over yonder.'

The new arrivals ravenously wolfed down the greasy fatback and beans. The other men seemed to have accepted the bona fides of the newcomers. Only Clu Sublette still harboured doubts. And it was his pride at having made a mistake that rankled.

After a mug of strong Arbuckles and a cigar apiece, Luther peered around. 'Where have you boys tethered your nags?' He had wandered over to the nosebags with the intention of feeding their own mounts.

'They are over behind those rocks,' answered Sublette in a menacing tone. 'Why do you want to know?'

'Have you already fed them?'

'They were grained and watered when we arrived here an hour ago,' replied a puzzled Brace Lincoln. 'What are you getting at?'

Luther was fingering a handful of grain when the sheriff walked across. 'You ever heard of Brackweed?'

The sheriff nodded, his eyes opening wide in shock. 'Of course, I have. Everybody knows about that darned stuff. You don't mean . . .'

'Better check your cayuses,' advised the worried man. 'This stuff will knock them out for a good twenty-four hours. Where did you get it?'

'The bags were hanging up in the livery stable.'

'The gang must have doctored the grain, figuring that was the only place in town that supplies it,' interjected

Luther. 'They knew that a posse would be formed up to go after them.'

Luther rubbed the lump on his head. 'Those guys sure ain't greenhorns when it comes to trickery and deception.'

No further explanation was needed as the men hustled over to the low cluster of rocks behind which their mounts were picketed. The sight that greeted them brought sharp intakes of breath followed by angry curses. All four horses were splayed out on the ground, alive but unable to continue the pursuit for at least a full day.

Lincoln was more annoyed at his own feckless incompetence. 'I should have checked the bags before we left. It just never occurred to me that they could have been tampered with.'

'You ain't wrong there,' muttered Sublette. The mordant aside was not disputed by any of the other posse members.

Luther gave the speaker a piercing glower of censure as he tried to assuage the lawman's chagrin. 'It wasn't your fault, Sheriff. I only noticed it when I was coming round after those galoots slugged me. They dropped some of the seeds on the floor. It didn't occur to me at the time. My head was all mussed up. You mentioning the nosebags brought it all back with a vengeance.'

The well-meaning reflection did little to make Brace Lincoln feel any better. 'Well, that's done for us,' grumbled Lincoln. 'We'll never catch them now.' He stood with the others, their doleful eyes morosely regarding the fallen horses.

Once again the Meacher Gang had outsmarted the law. For the second time, a posse had been thwarted, a lawman left wondering how he had been so dumb-witted. On the other hand, Lady Luck had yet again seen fit to favour the two avengers.

And they intended to take full advantage of any opportunity presented.

# CHAPTER NINE

# AMBUSH

Texas Red and his men were sitting round a camp-fire in a hollow formed by an old dried-up lake bed. Here they were safe from observation. Yet still the gang leader felt the need to exert caution. Lex Gantry had been sent up to the rim to keep watch. The sun was beginning to make its presence felt. Peeping above the line of Joshua trees enclosing the site, the golden ball quickly drove away the shadowy tentacles of night.

Overhead, bunches of white cumulus drifted by on a light breeze. On the far side of the glade, a family of curious prairie dogs were giving the visitors the once-over. All seemed well with the world.

The gang boss was feeling pleased with himself as he chewed on a stringy rabbit's leg shot by the Cimarron Kid. The meat was washed down with coffee laced with the last of the French brandy purloined from the Cody general store. He tossed the empty bottle at the watching group. A rancid laugh followed the nosey varmints as they scurried for cover.

The idea to mix brackweed with the regular grain in those nosebags had been an inspiration worthy of any military commander.

Five days had passed since the robbery at Casper. They had crossed the border into Colorado on the previous afternoon. Another week of steady riding should see them at their destination. Only then could they fully relax.

Jubal Kade appeared to read his mind. 'Where we headed, boss?' The thought of all that lovely dough just sitting idly in the two saddle-bags was starting to bug him. 'My ass is becoming a mite saddle sore with all this riding.'

Meacher's reaction to the query was a disparaging sneer. 'We ain't out of the woods yet. Not by a long chalk. A wire could have been sent out warning other tin-stars to be on the lookout for us. I won't feel safe 'til we reach Purgatory.' A warped smirk revealing yellow teeth followed as he threw the finished leg bone into the fire. The grease sizzled and spat. 'Only then will we be able to relax. And believe me, boys, that's the place to give us a real good time.'

'Where is this berg called Purgatory?' Cimarron butted in, opening the last tin of peaches. 'I've heard rumours that it's one hell of a wild place.'

Meacher was about to reply when Gantry called down from his lookout position.

'Hey, Red! Up here, quick!' The strident summons brought the three lounging outlaws to full alertness. Gantry's panicky holler was that of a man bearing ill tidings. 'We've got company. It must be that posse.'

'What the. . . !'

'You certain that grain was doctored properly, Red?' Kade interrupted with biting scepticism.

Meacher ignored the veiled accusation. He jumped to his feet and scrambled up the slope to join Gantry. The others were hard on his heels. A pointing finger from Gantry indicated the plume of dust. It was impossible to tell how many were in the group. But there was no doubt they were heading this way.

Meacher screwed up his eyes. His whole body stiffened. A rabid curse was torn from his lips.

'Darn it!' he railed, angrily slamming a bunched fist into the ground. 'That ain't dust from a posse. The brackweed must have done the trick all right. It's that damn blasted yellow stripe!'

'The other guy must be his partner,' snarled Kade, gritting his teeth in fury.

'How in thunderation did the critters wriggle their way out of that trap we set in Casper?' Meacher threw back.

Neither Kade nor the Cimarron Kid could offer any answers.

'They must've escaped from jail and are tracking us to get even,' suggested Gantry.

'Not to mention claiming the bounty on our heads,' added the grimacing Kid.

Meacher had seen enough. Arguments over the reasoning behind who was after them did not matter a jot now. The most important issue was to get away.

'Break camp,' he ordered. 'We need to leave here, pronto, and find some place to lay an ambush for those skunks.'

In less than five minutes, the gear was stashed and the four outlaws were back in the saddle. They left the hollow, continuing in a southerly direction. After an hour's hard riding, Meacher found the ideal spot for which he was searching. Forking left off the main trail, a narrow shelf of rock climbed steadily to round a promontory some hundred yards ahead. One man with a rifle would have an uninterrupted view of any approaching riders from the rocky enclave above.

'Jubal, reckon you can take those critters out from up yonder?' Meacher pointed to a cluster of rocks. He knew the shamed outlaw would relish his chance to get even.

'Be a pleasure!' was the outlaw's brisk reply. 'I got me some reckoning with those two bastards that involves a heavy dose of lead poisoning.' A menacing growl hissed from the brigand's twisted maw.

'Head up that shelf and find yourself a good spot,' Meacher proposed. 'We'll carry on along here. You can catch us up once those leeches have been dealt with.'

'Be like shooting fish in a barrel,' scoffed Kade.

Meacher's next order was for the Kid. 'Grab a piece of brushwood and rub out our tracks 'til we've crested that low hill ahead. That should keep them knuckleheads heading along the shelf to where Jube is waiting with his surprise reward.' He chuckled uproariously.

'That sure is a good plan, Red,' Gantry praised his *compadre*.

Meacher gave the compliment a nonchalant shrug. That's the reason I'm leader of this bunch and not you, old buddy, he thought, but he kept that to himself as the two men walked their mounts up the short grade.

Once the gang split up, Kade spurred his horse up the steeply canting shelf of rock. On rounding a vertical slab of rock jutting out from the shelf, a sharp eye scanned the arid terrain for the best place to set up an ambush. He soon found what he was looking for. When the shelf petered out, a flat sward was overlooked by an upthrust of broken sandstone. Access to the upper rim was by a narrow gully.

Dismounting, Kade led his horse up the stone-choked gully, then settled down hidden among the rocks above to await the arrival of his quarry.

The two pursuers arrived at the break of trail a half-hour later. They had ridden most of the night since leaving the Casper posse. The line of hoof prints continued ahead, forking left to climb up the narrow shelf. The Kid had done a good job in erasing the gang's tracks, effectively giving the false impression that this was the main trail.

Jay was in the lead, Luther following close behind. But something was bugging him. For the moment he could not quite place what was wrong. A furrowed brow indicated he was racking his brain for the solution to his dilemma. Then the truth struck home like a flash of lightning.

Red Meacher had omitted one vital consideration when crowing about his sure-fire winner of a plan.

'Hold up there, Jay,' Luther called out, dragging on the reins. The duo had just rounded the distinctive rocky outcrop when he voiced his concern. 'Something's not right here.' His narrowed gaze scanned the sandy terrain all around.

'What's on your mind?' asked the Bar Ys' cattleman.

'Take a look at those tracks we've been following.' Luther pointed out the set of horse prints that were clearly visible. 'Notice anything odd about them?'

Jay screwed up his face studying the line of sandy indents. He shook his head mystified by the conundrum posed by his partner. He was a practical cattle-man, not a logical thinker. 'Can't say I do,' he admitted.

'We're chasing a gang of at least three outlaws, maybe more. Yet there's only one set of tracks heading up here. What do you make of that?'

Jay's eyebrows lifted. 'Gee! I'd never have thought of that if'n you hadn't pointed it out,' he exclaimed. 'You'd make a good detective, buddy! Maybe the gang have split up around here, someplace?'

'Just what I was thinking,' murmured Luther in agreement half to himself. 'The obvious route would appear to have come this way. I never noticed when the prints of several horses suddenly ended, leaving just this one line. My betting is that the gang have brushed out the tracks further back and sent one man up yonder to act as a decoy.' He peered ahead but could see nothing to confirm his suspicions.

Jubal Kade was well hidden.

'So what do you think we should do?' asked Jay, acceding to his partner's apparent penchant for problem-solving of this kind.

His partner was given no chance to reply. Jay's horse reared up on its hind legs, frightened by the squirming of a rattlesnake in its path. It was that which saved Jay's life as the deep-throated cough of a rifle boomed out. The bullet struck his horse in the neck. Blood spurted from the killing shot, the stricken animal tumbling over, trapping its rider beneath.

The danger having been eradicated in an unexpected fashion, the snake slithered away, disappearing into the rocks. Luther leapt out of the saddle and dove behind the dead body of the horse just as another bullet thudded into its lifeless form. Jay was groaning. The weight of the big animal had landed full square on him.

'You all right, Jay?' It was a fruitless question made under extreme duress. Jay Barwise was clearly in pain.

'Reckon I could have broken some ribs,' was the croaked reply. 'Everything else seems OK.' His face contorted into an agonizing scowl when he tried to shift the heavy burden ensnaring him. He fell back, panting from the painful exertion.

It was fortunate that the fallen horse was providing cover from the hidden renegade. Nevertheless, they were pinned down and sitting ducks if'n they moved. Making sure he kept out of sight, Luther attempted to lever the heavy bulk of the horse up sufficiently for Jay to slide out. It was a stroke of good fortune that only the forequarters were holding Jay down rather than the bulky torso.

After much grunting and striving, Jay managed to haul himself out. He lay gasping. Each gulp of air into his tortured lungs brought further tooth-jarring groans.

Meanwhile, the gunman was continuing to rain bullets down on them at irregular intervals. Up above, Jubal Kade was cursing his bad luck. If'n that sidewinder hadn't butted in, he could have finished this job easily. He had also noticed that the other rider was the Bar Ys' ramrod and not, as previously assumed, Skip Jenner.

The reasoning behind this mystery defeated the outlaw's reckoning. It wasn't important, anyway. The main issue was to ensure they didn't continue the pursuit. Now he would have to wait until the critters made a move, which they surely would have to do eventually.

An hour drew on, then two. The sun had passed its zenith. They were now into the hottest part of the day.

Up here in the rocks, Kade had commandeered a shady recess from the relentless heat of the sun. Nearby was a small rock pool. Time was on his side. Down there in the open it must be like a fiery furnace. Give them another hour and the heat would drive them to take hopeless risks. That was when Jubal Kade would finish the job. He was relishing the moment when both these popinjays would be eradicated for good.

Luther was also acknowledging this unassailable fact. The relentless heat was sucking every last bit of moisture from their bodies. His own horse had wandered away out of the firing line. And to add insult to injury, Jay's water bottle had been punctured by a bullet. The life-giving elixir dribbled away, now nothing more than a dark stain in the sand.

Kade scooped up a hatful of water and doused himself. The cooling balm was like nectar to the gods. He sighed with pleasure. Taking a brief peep from between the rocks he could see the dead horse but not the two men secreted behind it. But what he did spot was the dark stain in the sand where one of his bullets had holed their canteen. He chuckled uproariously.

'You guys want some water?' he called out, scooping up another hatful and tossing it over the lip of the rocks. 'I got me a fine spring up here. Man, it's mighty cooling in this heat. Just come out with your hands held high. I'll let you have all you want. No charge.' Another hoarse cackle echoed down from the rocky citadel above.

Luther licked his dried lips. His tongue felt like a lump of leather in his mouth. But it was Jay who needed the water more. The guy was suffering badly. But what could he do?

Then he noticed the gully up which Kade had gone to mount his attack. If'n he could just reach the bottom of the cliff face, he would be unseen from above. An assault on the cragfast bastion would then be on the cards. He turned to Jay.

'How much ammo have you got left for that Henry?'

Jay considered the question. 'Reckon no more than ten rounds,' was his reply.

'That will have to be enough,' Luther mused.

'What do you have in mind?' Jay winced as he struggled to turn over.

Briefly, Luther explained his plan. 'You don't have to hit the bastard. Just keep his head down until I reach the gully.

'Anything's worth a try,' the injured man panted. His lips were blistered and raw. 'We can't stay here for much longer.'

Luther helped Jay into position, the carbine resting on the dead horse's neck. 'When I'm ready, I'll tap you on the shoulder. Start firing as fast as you can until the slide is empty. Praise be that I'll have made it over yonder by then.'

Shucking his hat and gun-belt, Luther stuck the Army Remington into his belt. With gritted teeth, he prepared to launch himself into the unknown. 'You ready?' The entreaty seemed to belong to someone else. Jay nodded.

A tap on the shoulder and the first shot rang out. Luther was on his feet racing like the wind across the short open tract of ground. Levering and firing for all he was worth was sheer agony for the rifleman. But he thrust the pain aside, forcing his body to ignore the shuddering recoil. All that mattered was for Luther to make it over to the gully unseen. Eyes tight shut, he just let fly. All too soon the hammer clicked on empty. A harsh silence suddenly enveloped the arena of conflict.

His head dropped, tortured lungs desperately sucking in the hot air. A wary peep round the side of the horse's head and he just had time to notice Luther disappearing up the gully.

He had made it!

Jay lay back. Sheer exhaustion was ready to claim both mind and body.

Meanwhile, Luther Pickett was wasting no time. Careful to avoid dislodging any stones, he crept silently up the narrow fissure. At the top, he gingerly crawled out on to a flat ledge of rock. Peering round, searching eyes tried to locate the outlaw's hideout. At first he could not see anything other than an untidy amalgam of rocks and salt bush.

Climbing a little higher up, he circled round to the right and soon came across the gunman's horse. The animal regarded him with a jaded stare before resuming its idle chewing. Luther moved towards the rim of the mesa where he suddenly came across the prone gunman lying beside the pool. Jubal Kade had his back to Luther. The guy's whole attention was focused on the dead horse below.

Luther cracked a half smile. Drawing his revolver he stepped down on to the ledge.

'Don't move a muscle, fella,' he snarled out. 'I'm just itching to take you down.' Kade's back stiffened. 'Now drop the rifle and push it away.' Once the gun was out of reach Luther gave his next order. It was delivered with a curt asperity. 'On your feet, and make it slow and easy. Hands in the air and no funny business.'

Kade obeyed. Thus far he had not uttered a word of protest. But his mind was racing. Initial shock at having been tricked had paralysed his movements. But now the hard-nosed cunning of the seasoned outlaw pushed to the fore. Slowly he turned to face his adversary, hands remaining by his side. A hang-dog expression implied that he had accepted defeat.

'You sure caught me out, Pickett,' the outlaw admitted, assuming a false air of approbation. 'Guess old Jubal ain't cut out for this sort of caper no more.'

'Drop your gun-belt!' Luther snapped out, ignoring the blether.

'Sure, sure,' muttered Kade in apparent surrender. His hands slid to the front buckle. An exaggerated sigh issued from the outlaw's sad-looking face.

Then, with a swiftness worthy of a striking rattler, he grabbed for the holstered revolver. The gun rose.

Luther sensed the abrupt move moments before it happened. The tightness around Kade's narrowed gaze gave him away. The hunter's revolver replied first, moments before a bullet zinged past his ear. It was not a killing shot, taking Kade in the shoulder.

The outlaw back-footed, a startled look of surprise planted on the leathery mush. Teetering on the threshold of the mesa rim, his arms windmilled frantically. Then he disappeared from view. Luther moved quickly to the edge.

The splayed-out body of the dead outlaw lay unmoving below. Luther felt his heart pumping. He felt, giddy, light-headed. For some the taking of a human life is easy. Luther Pickett did not count himself among that callous breed.

The sight of his partner waving from behind the dead horse brought him back from the brink. The movement snapped him out of the trance-like state just in time. Otherwise he would have been joining the deceased Jubal Kade strumming a harp – or maybe stoking up the fiery furnace.

He stumbled across to the rock pool and doused his head in the cooling liquid. The sudden jolt to the system brought him round sufficiently to descend the gully leading the outlaw's horse.

Jay was on his feet. One arm lay across his chest supporting the sore ribs. 'When I heard those shots, I figured the rat might have sussed your plan. Then I saw him plunge off the rim. You nearly followed him.'

'Guess it was the shock of it all,' muttered Luther. 'It's been a long time since I killed a man. And it don't get any easier, no matter that he was a thieving brigand.'

He handed over the outlaw's full canteen which Jay swallowed in a single draught. Luther made a sling out of the outlaw's spare shirt to bind up his partner's injury. Then he took Kade's horse and went in search of his own. It was more than an hour before he returned. By then, the day was far advanced so they decided to camp out. At least they now had extra rations.

Unfortunately, the outlaw's saddle-bags were devoid of the hold-up money. Another downer was that the rest of the gang were getting further away. And more delay would be required in the next town to get medical attention for Jay. So it was a somewhat morose duo who sat round the flickering embers of a fire that night. Drawing on stogies, they kept their own counsel, musing on the day's grim events and the mammoth task still to be accomplished.

Starlight bathed the harsh terrain in its silvery glow before they finally succumbed to the welcome embrace of Orpheus.

# CHAPTER TEN

# STAMPEDE!

Texas Red Meacher and his remaining two men made good progress as they headed south. The mountain country that characterized the central belt of Colorado was on their right. He made a point of avoiding the major settlement of Denver just in case their names and descriptions had been wired through.

Two days had passed and still Jubal Kade had not rejoined them. Cimarron kept looking behind, surveying their back trail. But there was no sign of Kade. He was becoming a mite jumpy. First it was Rubin Stagg, now Kade. One by one, the gang was getting slowly whittled down.

When he voiced his concern, Meacher shrugged off his apprehension. 'He'll be along. Like as not the guy's stopped off at some trading post to celebrate.'

'Too much fire water will have soused his brain.'

Gantry's crack brought a hoot of laughter from the boss.

Their levity did nothing to assuage the Kid's edginess. They were heading down the Black Squirrel when, for the umpteenth time that day, Cimarron glanced behind. On this occasion he spotted a plume of dust in the distance.

'Hey, boys, it must be Jubal!' he called out.

Meacher drew rein and looked back. He waited until the dust cleared. Then he mouthed a rabid curse.

'Some'n wrong, Red?' enquired Gantry.

'That ain't Kade's dust,' he exclaimed. 'It's that damned yellow stripe and his buddy. They must have done for him.'

'Those critters are like leeches that won't let go,' muttered Cimarron's anxiety-loaded voice.

Gantry was derisory of his dead colleague's ineffectiveness. 'I allus figured that jackass would make a mess of it,' he grumbled. 'I should have done the job myself.'

Meacher didn't seem at all fazed by the loss of Kade. 'That's one less to share with. All the more dough for us. We'll settle with those two for keeps soon enough. And next time I'll make certain they're dead, and stay dead.'

'How far behind are they?' stuttered the jumpy Kid.

'No more than an hour so we need to eat dust,' urged Meacher, digging his spurs in hard. The other two followed in his wake.

This was no time for relaxing. The assumption that Kade would have taken care of their predators was now shot to pieces. The realization dawned that danger was within striking distance. Heads down, the wind flattening the brims of their hats, the three fugitives galloped hell for leather towards the safety of a rocky escarpment a few miles ahead.

Close up, the Black Squirrel River faded to little more than a trickle, eventually disappearing into the base of the cliffs. At some point in the distant past when the twisting serpent was a more dominant force, the surging waters had carved out a deep canyon. A trail drive chuck wagon was drawn up to one side of the canyon.

Standing by the camp-fire was an old guy sucking on a corncob pipe. His negro assistant was stirring a blackened pot. They had come through from the opposite end of the canyon and were now awaiting the rest of the trail-driving crew.

The three outlaws hailed the cook but had no intention of stopping.

Pancake Tanner acknowledged their wave but added a note of caution that brought the gang to a halt. 'If'n you fellas are headed through Gooseneck Canyon, watch how you go. We have a large herd coming through and the boys are pushing them hard.'

'Much obliged for the warning, mister,' Meacher reciprocated.

He would have relished the chance to step down for a spell. That chow the old cook was preparing smelled real good. But those two varmints were hot on their tail. The gang boss smirked as he spurred off up Gooseneck Canyon. A scheme was being hatched in his devious mind to scotch those pesky irritants once and for all.

As they pressed further into the confines of the narrow pass, the Kid swung round in his saddle. 'Those jaspers are closing up, Red,' he called out. Fear was clearly evident in the young tough's panicky outburst. 'They'll be on us soon.'

'That's just fine, Kid. Let them come.'

Meacher's reaction was too casual as far as the Kid was concerned. And to add insult to injury, he could hear the thundering of hoofs coming down the canyon from up ahead. 'What we gonna do?' he bleated. 'Those steers will be on us soon.'

The panic-stricken whingeing was ignored. Another two minutes passed. Then Meacher spotted what he had been searching for. The steady rumble of the approaching herd was increasing rapidly. Then suddenly, the lead steers hove out of the billowing cloud of dust that filled the narrow rift of the Gooseneck. The booming roar rebounded off the canyon walls. When he saw the approaching herd, Meacher signalled for the others to follow him off the trail up a steep grade to the right. This was just what he had been hoping for.

'Up here!' he yelled above the deafening crash of the rumbling beasts which were still some way down the neck of the canyon.

But the rough nature of the terrain had loosened the ties binding the heavy saddle pack fastened to Cimarron's cantle. The leather bag slid off.

'The bag's gone!' the Kid screamed. The thought of losing all that dough after all they'd been through overshadowed the clear danger of its retrieval. Cimarron dragged his snorting horse to a halt as the bag tumbled back down the slope. 'I'm going down for it.'

'Don't be a durned fool!' Gantry rapped out. 'You'll be trampled to death down there.'

But pure greed had raised its ugly head. Disappearing greenbacks floated before Cimarron's eyes. The Kid was not for turning. He plunged down the slope. The lead steers were only moments away when he reached the fallen bag and grabbed it up.

He tried to dodge the first of the beeves, which were moving at a brisk lick. And he would have made it had his horse not slipped on the loose shale. That split second signed his death warrant. He was thrown to the ground. Heads down, the foremost critters continued their remorseless progress, unheeding of the stricken human.

'Aaaarrrrgggh!'

The ululating shriek sent a shiver down Gantry's spine as his one-time sidekick was stamped into the ground. The cry was cut short as the mindless trudge of beating hoofs rumbled along the canyon.

Meacher ignored the Kid's sudden demise. He had other things on his mind. Jamming the Winchester into his shoulder, he cranked the lever of the repeater. A half dozen bullets were loosed at the leading steer.

The accurate shots clipped the wide horns. Bits flew off like hornets buzzing around a dead lizard.

The effect was momentous, and just what Meacher had expected. The lead steer raised its head and bellowed at the strip of blue sky overhead. A circling bald eagle responded with a strident quawk, quawk. Slavering mouths gaped wide in utter panic as the whole herd instantly picked up on their leader's terror. In the beat of an eagle's wing, their pace had speeded up.

A fully-fledged stampede was under way.

Meacher howled with glee. 'Now ain't that a perty sight,' he chortled, slapping his partner on the back as the last steers trundled past leaving the mangled corpse of the Cimarron Kid behind. The bag with his brimming contents was nowhere to be seen. The hoofs of a thousand hurtling beasts had totally destroyed it. Only the odd flutter of an escaping bill was left of the hold-up reward.

Meacher scowled. The Kid's demise was of little concern to him. But the loss of the dough certainly was. But he soon recovered. They still had most of it left, a substantial bounty.

'Don't worry, Lex,' he breezed, putting the second part of his plan into action. 'All the more for us!'

Gantry was perplexed and not a tad nervous. He had heard those words before from his old buddy. They were beginning to haunt him. And now there were two. Was Texas Red intending to erase him from the picture at some point in the near future? Gantry promised himself to keep a wary eye on his partner from here on.

Back down the canyon, the two pursuers had also heard the shots. Jay immediately cottoned to what had occurred.

'Those buzzards must have set off a stampede to run us down,' he hollered. 'Let's get out of here while we can.'

The two men swung their mounts around just as the herd came charging round the bend up ahead. Jay was still in a weakened state. His chest was throbbing like the devil. Luther slapped his partner's horse on the rump, urging the frightened animal to pick up the pace. He followed close behind as they both galloped off back the way they had come.

Engrossed in a full scale charge, the herd was now unstoppable. Jay knew all about these. A stampede was the most feared of all adversities faced by cattlemen. And this one was a right humdinger. The rampaging beasts were gaining on them. It was now a matter of pure survival.

'Faster, Jay,' yelled Luther, struggling to keep the alarm out of his voice. 'Fall off that cayuse now and you'll be nought but a smear on the ground.'

It was lucky that they had only just entered Gooseneck Canyon. Luther could see the entrance up ahead. He urged them both on with spirited encouragement. No more than fifty yards separated them from the berserk herd when at last they broke free of the stifling confines.

Once clear of the canyon, Jay forced his tired body to assume control. This was a situation he knew needed to be dealt with immediately. Otherwise the cattle would run and run until they were nothing but skin and bone, if'n they lasted that long. And he was the expert. As a cattleman he owed it to the ramrod in charge of the herd to save his livelihood.

'We need to turn them,' he informed Luther, drawing his pistol. 'Get them milling in a circle.' He swung to face the charging herd as it emerged from the canyon. With guns firing into the air and hats waving and slapping at the crazed animals, it was touch and go whether the manoeuvre would succeed.

But Jay Barwise had participated in numerous drives with his father on herds driven up the Texas trails. That was before they moved to Wyoming. He was confident of being able to turn them – eventually. Just so long as his incapacitated torso held out.

'Yah! Yah! Yah! Turn, you sons of the trail.'

Urgent howls of lively determination accompanied their frantic endeavour to swing the onward rush. Every jolt and shudder brought a pained wince to his strained features. Stamping and hollering amidst the clouds of yellow dust, the cattle spread out across the open sward. Two men alone stood little chance of halting the panic-stricken rush.

But they were not alone. Pancake Tanner and his assistant Rooster Joe were still sitting on the chuck wagon awaiting the rest of the crew. Witnessing the alarming prospect of a stampede, they joined in the mêlée adding to the cacophony. It was their involvement that swung the initial action in favour of the human masters. Once the back markers of the herd had spilled out of Gooseneck Canyon, the main bunch of drovers was able to add their skilful direction to the chaotic affray.

An hour later they had finally brought the milling beasts under control. It had been a close-run thing. The cattle were herded into a circle a quarter mile wide where they soon settled down. Thankfully, only one man had been injured when his horse broke a leg in a gophor hole. The drover was plucked to safety by a nearby flank rider. No such luck for the stricken animal, which was swiftly dispatched by the ramrod.

'The name's Gil Rossiter.' The big rangy guy held out a gloved hand. 'I'm trail boss for the Tumbling T ranch out of San Angelo, Texas. I owe you guys a heap of thanks for turning those critters.' His weathered face creased in a look of puzzlement. 'Mind telling me what happened? We heard some shots. Then the whole herd started out on the hoof.'

Luther filled him in with the details as he saw them.

'So, you reckon the stampede was started deliberately, hoping to get rid of you boys?' Luther nodded. 'Didn't see hide nor hair of them as we came through.' The ramrod scratched at his matt of yellow-dusted hair. 'They must have pulled off the trail half way up that branch canyon I noticed.'

But Luther's main concern now was for Jay Barwise, who had fallen off his horse. Two rannies carried him over to the chuck wagon where Pancake, a proficient amateur medic as well as a sound cook, was able to patch him up.

'You're in luck, young fella,' he announced, after securing a tight bandage around the injured man's aching body. 'No broken bones in there. Just bruised ribs. Keep that bandage on for another week and you'll be as fine as a new colt.'

Jay emitted a deep sigh of relief, mumbled his thanks then, totally exhausted, he fell into a deep sleep.

When Pancake announced that he had spoken to the

two outlaws, Luther asked him for a description. 'Only thing I noticed was that one had thick red hair and a beard.'

Next morning, following a good night's rest, both Luther and Jay were eager to be on their way. When Gil Rossiter learned that it was Robson Barwise's son who had prevented a wholesale catastrophe, he was more than willing to help the two avengers.

'Ain't never met your pa,' he said, 'but his reputation is well-known down in Texas. We've been pushing this herd north up the Goodnight-Loving trail for the last two months. Word is that the army at Fort Laramie are paying good money for Texas beef.'

Jay was able to confirm Rossiter's claim.

'That brand of your'n is almost as famous as the man himself,' the ramrod waxed lyrical. 'Anything I can do for you boys, just say the word.'

'We could do with a couple of fresh horses to catch up with those skunks,' Luther posited, 'so long as that ain't stretching your remuda.'

'Sure thing, boys. Help yourselves,' breezed Rossiter. 'We have a couple of fine Arab stallions in amongst those tough mustangs. You're mighty welcome to take them.'

Following a hearty breakfast from Pancake, who also re-stocked their saddle packs, the duo said their good-byes and headed off.

# CHAPTER ELEVEN

# CARRIZO INSURANCE POLICY

Meacher and Gantry made good progress across the rolling plains of south-east Colorado. The meandering Purgatoire River was crossed as the sun was dipping low towards the horizon. Just beyond lay the Carrizo Trading Post, where they intended resting up for the night.

'Good fortune sure gave us a helping hand when we ran into that trail herd,' Meacher enthused as they drew up outside the rickety shack.

'Not so good for Cimarron,' grunted his partner.

'Tough on him, maybe,' agreed Meacher, responding with an apathetic shrug. 'But that's how it goes in this game. Just think of all that lovely dough.' He tapped his saddle-bag, then pointed to a line of serrated ramparts to the south. 'That's Black Mesa,' he added. 'No Man's Land lies on the far side. Once we're over those hills, nobody can touch us.'

Meacher oozed confidence, certain they had effectively thwarted any further pursuit. But ever the caution dude, he still intended to make doubly sure with the help of the half-breed running the place.

A shady character of dubious motives, Sad-Eye Villa acted as a sort of intermediary between renegade Comanche bucks and ne'er-do-wells fleeing from the law. Both factions were frequent visitors. And between them there existed a tentative truce. The outlaws were tolerated as they paid well for 'services rendered'. The Indians who had broken from the main tribes had no compunction in cocking a snook at the white-man's law and, indeed, their own kind.

Three braves lounged outside the post. They were smoking cigars and drinking watered-down liquor.

'Is Sad-Eye in?' Meacher asked. One of the Indians slung a thumb over his shoulder. The newcomers angled through the door into the dim interior. The trader was at that very moment doctoring some bottles. So intent was he on not spilling any of the diluted concoction that he failed to heed the arrival of the new customers.

Meacher sneered at the devious trickery being performed.

'Well, what have we here?' he rasped out. The trading-post owner almost jumped out of his skin and dropped the half-filled bottle. 'I hope you ain't intending to serve us with that slop. It might obstruct your continued good health.' The outlaw's hand rested on the shiny gun butt of his right-hand pistol.

Sad-Eye spluttered a garbled imprecation, then quickly hid the incriminating evidence below the counter. A nervous laugh attempted to brush off his chicanery.

The Carrizo trader had earned his curious nickname following a knife fight with a rustler who had insulted Villa's Comanche mother. The skunk had paid with his life. But not before he had inflicted a serious wound now clearly evident down the breed's left cheek. After knitting together, the scar had pulled the adjoining peeper down giving Villa a lob-sided appearance.

'Texas Red, my old friend,' he prattled trying to ingratiate himself back into the favour of the ruthless outlaw. 'Would I do that to you?' A shrug and a wry smirk attempted to deny any such antics towards his friends. Then in a lower voice he said, 'It's specially reserved for those jiggers outside. Can't hold their liquor. And unlike guys with taste such as yourselves, they can't tell the difference.'

'Cut the flannel, Sad-Eye, and give us some of the proper stuff,' Meacher snapped, stepping across the threshold into the gloomy interior.

'Of course, of course,' the proprietor burbled as he reached for a bottle of real Scotch from the back shelf. 'Only the best for Texas Red Meacher and his friends.'

'Still up to your old tricks, eh?' Meacher charged, sinking the fine whiskey and pushing the glass back for a refill. 'Guess these will be on the house then.' The blunt declaration was issued as a statement of fact rather a question. Hard eyes bore into the skinny trader challenging him to object.

A toadying leer and the glasses were topped up. No money changed hands.

'So what are you doing in Carrizo, Red? I haven't seen you for' – the trader thought for a moment – 'why, must be all of two years.'

'We're heading down to Purgatory for some much needed rest and relaxation,' came back the breezy reply. 'But we might need a little help from you to make certain we get there unscathed.' He drew a wad of bills from his pocket and carefully counted off a handful. 'It'll be worth your while. And you might not even have to do anything. We just want some added insurance in case it's needed.'

Meacher noted the avaricious gleam as Villa's squinting gaze fastened on to the banknotes. The small heap contained more dough than the trader made in a month running this fleapit. He scooped it up. The outlaw's mouth twisted in a dry smirk of predictability. He knew Sad-Eye Villa of old. And money always talks big time.

Two cigars were extracted from a humidor. He lit them up and handed one to Gantry, appreciating the fine aroma.

'What is it you want me to do?'

There was no hesitation in Villa's grasping response. The outlaw then went on to describe only those recent events he considered necessary for Villa to know. The crux was that should their two dogged pursuers somehow have managed to trail them down here, Villa would prevent them continuing the chase.

'Have no fear, Red. I'll see to it that you reach Purgatory without interruption,' Villa assured his visitors. 'Broken Nose and his associates are well versed in removing obstructions in the way of progress.' He poured out some more whiskey, sealing the bargain. 'To a successful and enjoyable vacation!'

The three cronies raised their glasses. 'I'll sure drink to that,' Meacher warbled.

The next morning, the two outlaws swung into the saddle.

'Likely those cattle drovers will have had to scrape those skunks off the trail. In which case you've earned a hundred bucks for doing nothing. But if'n they do happen to turn up. . . .'

Villa nodded as he interrupted. 'Rest assured, Tex. My boys will make sure they get no further.' The two men shook hands.

Four days passed before the hunters arrived at Carrizo. Their journey had not been straightforward. After leaving Gil Rossiter and the Tumbling T, they had made for the nearest settlement.

La Junta was on a bend of the Arkansas River. Here the gentle swell of the meandering watercourse narrowed and was at its shallowest. As such it provided a safe crossing point for the Santa Fe Trail.

Both men were in need of a much-needed overhaul. High on their list of priorities was a new set of duds. Luther especially wanted to be rid of the Union britches and officer's hat, which had become a yoke around his neck. And judging by the sniffy noses of the local women, baths were also a major requirement.

Jay was able to have his badly bruised ribs professionally attended to. The doctor recommended he rest up for at least a week. But there was no time for that luxury. With every day spent in La Junta, their quarry was getting further away.

Clad in fresh range garb and smelling less like saddle bums, they were able to blend into the town's landscape. They soon discovered, however, that any enquiries regarding the quickest route to Purgatory were met with alarm and suspicion.

'The only jaspers heading that way are either bandits or army deserters,' snorted the owner of the Animas Saloon. A challenging regard defied the two newcomers to answer the implied accusation. A half dozen local citizens also squared off in support of Abner Lucas. The atmosphere in the saloon was cooler than a jug of iced tea. 'So what's your interest in that den of thieves?'

Luther vehemently denied any lawless endeavour on their part. And when he mentioned they were tracking a red-headed jasper and his partner, the initial frosty reception visibly thawed.

'Those two rats stole a couple of horses from my stable,' interposed the liveryman. 'I only found out when two broken-down crocks were left in their place. The scurvy low-lives even had the nerve to leave a note.' He pulled the offending missive from his back pocket and slapped it down on the bar top. It read Fair exchange is no robbery.

'Sounds like Texas Red Meacher, all right,' averred

Luther. 'That guy is more cunning than a snake-oil salesman.' He then went on to briefly outline the events that had brought them on this long ride to Purgatory.

Once the truth was explained over a few drinks in the Animas Saloon, Abner Lucas was effusive in his desire to help.

'Head south-east across the Otero Flats,' he advised, refusing payments for their drinks. 'It's a tough ride but the shortest way. On the far side is the only human habitation. The Carrizo Trading Post is run by a half-breed Mex-Comanche by the name of Sad-Eye Villa. You'll need to stock up on supplies there. But watch out for Villa. He'd sell his own mother if'n it turned a profit.'

'Looks like him and Meacher are two peas in a pod,' commented Jay Barwise.

The ride across the burning crystalline white flats was no picnic. A bleak wasteland, the dazzling reflection of the sun hurt their eyes. And shade was at a distinct premium. Only the odd clump of creosote bush and blue-stemmed buffalo grass disturbed the unbroken aridity. Hawks and woodpeckers occasionally flew by overhead. Yet still jack rabbits, wood rats and the ubiquitous coyote managed to flourish in this alien environment. Not so humans, of which there was nary a sign.

So it was with mixed feelings that the weary travellers eventually sighted the lone cluster of hutments that comprised Carrizo.

The two men approached the trading post warily. Three idling Comanches studied the newcomers with hostile eyes. The owner of the post stepped down to greet his new customers. Sad-Eye Villa was all smiles. Any sign of duplicity was effectively concealed behind the obsequious kowtowing manner.

'Welcome to Carrizo, strangers,' gushed the half-breed, flapping his arms. 'Step inside for some much-needed refreshment. First drink is on the house.'

Luther and his buddy were not taken in by the false display of bonhomie. Nonetheless, they played along.

'Much obliged,' replied Luther as they dismounted. 'We could sure do with something to eat as well after that trek over the Flats.'

'Tortillas and beef chilli all right?' Villa asked, ushering them inside the post. 'My woman is the best cook around.' A corpulent Comanche squaw wandered out of the kitchen toting a large hunk of bread, which she silently deposited on the table.

'We could also do with some fresh supplies,' posited Jay.

'Give your order to Broken Nose here,' said Villa gesturing to the surly buck hovering nearby. 'He'll sort you out.'

'And maybe you could give us some information?'

The question hung in the air as Villa considered the request.

'Now that, señor, depends on what you wish to know,' he muttered, pasting a fawning smirk on his oily face.

'Have two jaspers passed through here in the last few days?' enquired Luther, shovelling down the somewhat dubious food presented to him by the Indian cook. 'One of them is a big dude sporting a red beard.'

Villa considered the query, purposefully scratching his black greasy hair. 'Nobody of that description has come to Carrizo.' He turned to pose the same question to the woman. She merely shook her head. 'Sorry, we can't help you. Are these hombres friends of your'n?' The innocently posed query was a more searching probe.

'Just some guys we need to have words with,' said Jay, refusing to be drawn. 'Pity you ain't seen them.'

Villa shrugged, removing their empty plates.

Then Jay's attention was drawn back to his partner by a boot nudging his own under the table. He peered across at Luther, who surreptitiously leaned his head to the right. Jay followed his partner's directive. And there it was, scattered across the floor over in the corner – long clippings of red hair.

Tex Meacher had clearly availed himself of a barber's job, doubtless conducted by the squaw. Luckily for them, she had forgotten to clean up afterwards. So now they knew that Meacher and his sidekick had passed through here, and recently.

But why had Sad-Eye Villa denied any knowledge of them? The obvious answer was that Meacher had bribed him. The devious outlaw was once again attempting to thwart their plans to capture him.

'What do you make of that?' Jay asked his buddy.

'My guess is that Meacher has paid that scheming rat to rub us out. And I reckon he'll get his Indian buddies to do the job.' Luther stared ahead, his steely look intent on countering any subterfuge. He spat into the dust. 'Lowdown critters like that let others do all their dirty work. From here on we're gonna have to watch our backs until they make their move.'

Soon after Luther and Jay had left Carrizo, the trader summoned the Indian leader inside the store. Broken Nose stubbed out the butt of his cigar and joined him. A glass of whiskey was pushed towards him. Nose sank it in a single gulp. No intimation registered on his swarthy features that it was anything other than the genuine article.

Villa's face broke into an ingratiating smile. He had these gullible saps right where he wanted them.

The Indian had long straggly hair tied back with a bandana. He was clad in elaborately embroidered buckskins fringed at the edges. Around his neck hung an array of charms to ward off evil spirits. The renegade might have forsaken his native Comanche ways, but he still held on to certain mystical elements passed down through the generations by the tribal medicine man.

'You have work for Broken Nose?' the Indian punched out in a deep drawl.

'I sure do, buddy. And there'll be ten bucks in it for you and your pals, plus a jug of my best firewater.' Villa topped up the Indian's glass. 'You happy with that?'

The Indian just stood there, legs apart. His granite features remained taciturn. Then he replied. 'Make that one jug each and is deal.'

Villa gave the conditional response a leery frown. 'You drive a hard bargain, Nose. But guess I can accommodate you.' He held out a hand, which the Indian shook. The deal that he had expected all along was struck. Broken Nose departed to inform his associates of their good fortune. But it was Villa who was the clear winner.

# CHAPTER TWELVE

# NO MAN'S LAND

That night Luther and his partner camped beside a shallow creek in the lee of Black Mesa. Following a simple meal they talked over their plans. The following day would see them crossing the line. It would be *adiós* to civilized America as they passed into a strip of land beyond the reach of any help from the law should things go awry. It was a daunting prospect that saw each man cocooned within his own thoughts as they sat smoking in the flickering firelight.

The moon was high overhead. Its gentle silvery glow imbued the scene with an idyllic aura. Jay checked the horses and re-kindled the fire with fresh wood to deter any nocturnal predators. A final check was made to ascertain that they were alone. Then both men settled down for the night.

Silence enfolded the camp-site. Only the distant haunting refrain of a night owl disturbed the serenity of the scene.

Yet all was not as it appeared. As the shining disc drifted across the night-sky, its comforting brilliance faded. Suddenly the friendly shadows were transformed into bizarre contortions to which an over-active imagination might easily attach all manner of macabre connotations. And they would not have been far removed from reality.

The moon's ethereal glow revealed the stealthy movement of black shadows creeping silently towards the camp. They halted behind a cluster of rocks and three sets of hostile eyes studied the layout.

The fire had died down to a smouldering bed of ash. On either side were two huddled forms wrapped in bed rolls. They lay unmoving, oblivious that they were being watched by marauding prowlers who meant them harm.

Broken Nose grunted his approval. All was as it should be. The prey was completely at their mercy. He signalled for his men to stand up and notch their arrows. A brisk nod and the twang of bowstrings loosed the deadly missiles towards their supine targets. Their aim was spot on. The Comanche shafts thudded into the blanketed humps.

Howling familiar tribal war chants, all three renegades rushed down the slope. Tomahawks were raised aloft ready to bury them deep into the supine bundles, dispatching them to eternity. Once, twice, three times, the deadly blades fell.

Then a rapid-fire series of pistol shots rang out. The darkness was torn apart by orange tongues of flame lancing from two gun barrels.

The attackers didn't stand a chance, nor were they given one. Enough fire light remained to present the intended victims with perfect targets. Luther and his buddy stepped out from cover and advanced across the open sward. Guns blazed with unremitting fury until none of the cowardly bushwhackers remained alive.

Smoke drifted from the hot barrels as the two men quickly checked the accuracy of their shooting. Standing still, shoulders heaving and guns still gripped tightly in clenched hands, they breathed long and hard, allowing time to release the stiffness from their taut bodies.

'I reckon that deserves a tot of whiskey in our coffee,' Jay declared, moving across to where the black pot stood on a wire grill beside the fire. The bottle was soon emptied along with the coffee, enabling them both to fall into a dreamless slumber. Both victors and vanquished in the brief skirmish lay sprawled out side by side.

Attracted by the smell of death, a sneaky coyote gingerly sniffed at one of the corpses. A drunken snort from one of the sleeping men sent it scurrying away. There would be plenty of time later for a more protracted investigation.

It was only when the winners awoke the next morning nursing sore heads that the full and bitter truth of the conflict struck home. They quickly packed up and departed from the grisly scene, leaving the corpses for wandering scavengers to remove at their leisure. Perched on a nearby shelf the coyote howled at the rising sun – a mournful howl that summoned the other members of the pack to come a-running.

Soon the two riders were climbing into the foothills of Black Mesa. By early afternoon they were descending the far side. Although no sign-post announced their arrival, both men knew they had entered the anomalous tract referred to as No Man's Land.

Ahead of them stretched a flat grassy wilderness. Once the foothills were left behind, trees were in short supply allowing buffeting winds to hammer across the open plain. The Homestead Act of 1862 had allowed settlers to come into the unoccupied territory. The dearth of trees meant that turf houses had to be built. These people became known as 'sodbusters'. Farming the land, they added to their fragile incomes by grinding down the bones of dead buffalo and making moonshine.

The land was also ideal for cattle-ranching. Conflict between the two factions was always simmering close to the surface, frequently erupting into violence. With no official authority to quell the unrest, men took the law into their own hands. Justice was swift and final. Most people saw this as the best solution to avoid lengthy court cases and expense.

Various towns sprang up in which anything went. Purgatory became the most renowned, or infamous depending on whose opinion was sought. It operated twenty-four hours a day with no holidays. Constant merriment catering to the transient population brought wealth to the suppliers of liquor, girls and gambling.

To keep the outlaws happy, and their lawless gains within the precincts of Purgatory, a host of outdoor entertainments were provided, including horse-racing, boxing and wrestling matches, together with shooting contests.

There was no shortage of takers as outlaws and desperadoes seeking a safe haven flocked to this lawless land. One imaginative reporter penned the immortal headline – God's Land? No, Man's. And so the name that most folk associated with the unoccupied territory was born. And it stuck.

Now that they were getting closer to their objective, a tense atmosphere settled over the two men. Talk was limited, their minds focused on what lay ahead. Neither had visited Purgatory before. Although Jay had passed close when coming up the trail with his father all those years before.

Robson had strictly forbidden his men from sampling the lurid delights about which they had all heard rumours. Not that he was a Bible-bashing Puritan like some of his fellow ranchers. Caution dictated his order. The cattle came first and he was worried that some of the hands would fail to return.

After all, if the reports passed down the trails were to be believed, Purgatory was a town where anything went. Temptations would be rife, impossible for some to resist. And where no law prevailed, the sky was the limit.

'Have you figured out how we're going to deal with these varmints?' Jay posed the question that had also been on Luther's mind. 'This place is wide open. Meacher is sure to be amongst his own kind. And with no official law enforcement, we could be putting our heads in the lion's mouth just riding in there unprepared.'

'We need to blend into the landscape,' Luther suggested before passing the problem back to his partner, 'so that nobody gives us a second glance. Going in with shooting irons on display will attract attention. Those guys will be looking us over to see whether we pose a threat to their continued well-being. Any bright ideas?'

Jay thought for a moment. Then an idea struck him. His face lit up. Luther picked up on his buddy's newfound optimism. 'Reckon I have at that,' he murmured.

'You gonna share this brainwave?'

'It's what you said about not posing a threat. We have to look totally harmless. Then the lawless scum that inhabit these towns will ignore us.' A beaming smile challenged his partner to figure out his own logical solution. Luther's face remained blank. 'It's simple,' Jay continued. 'Who could be more down at heel than a simple Mexican peon. This strip of land was the northern most part of Mexico before it was annexed by Texas. There are still a considerable number of them living around here.'

'You're a genius,' Luther congratulated his partner. 'Why didn't I think of that?'

'Some of us have it up here.' Jay tapped his head, just managing to evade the playful punch. 'And just over that ridge is a horse farm run by Mañuel Ortez.'

'Isn't there an Ortez works for your pa?' asked Luther now thoroughly attuned to this highly unusual plan.

'That's his son, Louis. He's assistant wrangler with the Bar Ys.' Jay then went on to explain the circumstances. 'Mañuel saved Pa's life when a rogue bull charged him. He only managed to get out the way because Mañuel stepped into the open. He was waving a red blanket to divert the critter's attention. Poor guy was nearly gored himself. But it allowed Pa to scramble out of reach.'

'Sounds like a straight-up sort of guy.' Luther was impressed.

'Pa insisted on buying some of his horses. He also said that when Louis was of age, there would be a job for him anytime up in Wyoming. The kid arrived last year and has settled in just fine working alongside Bronco Travis. Maybe you recall him?'

Luther thought for a moment. 'Yep,' he drawled out. 'A small wiry runt, but real smart with a lariat.'

'That's him.'

'So let's go pay this hero of a father that visit,' said Luther, spurring off.

The ranch was no more than a sod house dug into a low hill. The roof comprised a line of ridge poles with plum and chokecherry brush supporting more buffalo grass turf. Wild prairie roses and morning glory provided a colourful adornment. To one side was another sod building used for storage. Even the corral where the horses were kept was made from the sod. Of trees there was no sign in any direction. In addition to horses, Mañuel Ortez had planted open fields of squash, beans and corn. A wind pump had been erected to draw water from a hundred feet down.

The man himself together with a young boy was wrestling with a plough pulled by two horses. Spring planting was well under way. He stopped on noting the arrival of two riders heading in from the north. A cautious hand dropped to the old cap and ball Navy Colt that was always tucked into his belt.

'No need for that, Mañuel,' Jay call out raising his own hands to show they came in peace. 'Don't you recognize me?'

Ortez pushed back his sombrero to study the newcomers more closely. Squinting and frowning, he struggled to identify the speaker. Bulging eyes then indicated that the nickel had dropped.

'Señor Barwise!' The Mexican's mouth fell open in surprise. 'Is it really you after all this time? Must be all of erm . . a lot of years. You have changed, *señor.*'

'That's because I've grown up. I was a lot younger when we passed through here back in '66. And there's no need for the formality. Call me Jay.' Then he waved an arm towards his partner. 'And this is my buddy Luther Pickett.'

The farmer nodded to Luther. 'You are both welcome to the ranch of Mañuel Ortez.' Then he turned to the staring boy. 'And this is my son Pablo. Go tell Mamma that we have guests and to prepare the spare room. You will eat with us and stay the night, I hope? There is much to talk over.'

'Be glad to, Mañuel. And I hope that Maria is in good health and still turning out those mouth-watering enchiladas.'

Ortez laughed. 'That is for you both to judge. Why don't you ride up to the house and introduce yourselves?' In the meantime, Pablo had not moved. He just stood there, ogling these two dust-caked tough guys. 'Hurry, hurry, silly one!' his father chided, shooing the boy into motion.

That soon jerked Pablo from his reverie. Hallooing with glee, the skinny kid bounded off towards the farmhouse.

Much was discussed about the times in between their last meeting. In those days, No Man's Land had only just been opened up. Since then it had become a haven for all manner of riff-raff. The troublesome factions had not bothered Mañuel and his family thus far. But other farmers had been attacked so he was taking no chances. Hence the gun continually secreted about his person.

Jay was able to reassure him that his oldest son was doing fine on the Bar Ys spread and intended returning for a visit down here after the autumn steer cull.

Inevitably, the talk shifted to the duo's arrival in the unassigned territory. That was when Luther revealed the dire circumstances that had brought them south all the way from distant Wyoming. Mañuel warned them that the wanton reputation for violence and debauchery that Purgatory had acquired was no figment of the imagination.

'So, how can I help?' Ortez asked, eager to lend his support.

'We need some form of disguise to enter the town in secret. So no one will give us a second glance,' said

Luther. 'Jay here figured that you could supply us with Mexican working duds. Loose fitting to conceal our hardware.'

'No problem. We have plenty of spare gear. And large straw hats to hide your faces.' Ortez called over to his wife, who was doling out large second helpings of pumpkin pie. 'Maria, sort our *amigos* out with suitable clothing for their mission. We will then have a dress rehearsal.'

They all laughed when the two men strutted out of the bedroom clad in their new duds. 'No arrogant posturing, *amigos*,' cautioned Ortez. 'You need to adopt the downtrodden manner of the *peon*.' Jay and Luther hunched their shoulders in the well-known bearing that they all recognized. More laughter followed.

The two men regretted having to adopt this humiliating and degrading disguise that was an everyday feature of life for Mañuel's fellow countrymen. Unfortunately, it was essential if their deception was to be successful.

Underneath the good nature, however, there was an underlying sense of nervousness in the air, now that the finale of their quest was within sight.

Next morning, the two men left the farm with Mañuel Ortez and his family's good wishes. The future was now in their hands. Only time and good fortune would tell if a final redemption would be achieved.

# CHAPTER THIRTEEN

# PURGATORY

The cluster of shacks and hutments hove out of the early morning mist. Red Meacher and his buddy drew their horses to a halt. For five long minutes they just stared at the swelling township. On the outskirts, much scaffolding indicated the rapidity of growth being enjoyed by what was becoming a major settlement.

Purgatory had originally been named White City, then Beer City. It had grown to pre-eminence among the lawless dives scattered across No Man's Land by the time Meacher and his sidekick arrived.

The more recent appendage of Purgatory came about when unofficial town marshal Lew Bush was shot and killed by his lady friend, Pussy Cat Nell. Nell ran the Yellow Snake Saloon. It was the biggest and most popular of its kind in the town with the upper floor devoted to more earthy entertainments. The girls hailed from over the border in Liberal. They operated on a two-week shift system and were regularly brought in by horse-drawn hack.

It was with one of these girls that Nell accused her lover of dallying. Disregarding his excuses, she awaited his arrival, then blasted the poor sap with both barrels of her shotgun. The victim was not particularly missed as he had been more of a figurehead than a purveyor of law and order – in addition to which, he had operated a rustling racket on the side.

The self-elected mayor of Beer City, Barney Kruger, was playing poker at the time of the shooting. He almost jumped out of his skin when the sudden explosion chopped aside the regular saloon cacophony. The table went over, gambling chips scattered across the floor.

'What in thunder is this place coming to?' he shouted, angrily. 'It's like being trapped in Purgatory!'

The name stuck. It had an edge that appealed to the warped humour of the clientele. They enjoyed being able to delight others of their kind in different parts of the country about this berg where anything goes and the Devil plays all the best tunes.

'So here we are,' murmured Lex Gantry. His mouth hung ajar. Eyes transfixed, he just starred at the drab huddle of buildings. Was this the Shangri-la with which he had become so enthused? It didn't look much. Since they had crossed the border, Meacher had been regaling his buddy about this hell's-a-poppin' refuge from the law. So his doubts were expressed with care. 'I guess, like the best type of dame, there must be more to it than mere looks.'

'You're right there, buddy.' Meacher was more upbeat. 'Never judge a book by its cover. Sample what's on offer afore you voice an opinion.' He was not offended. Similar thoughts had gripped his own innards on first sighting the notorious den of iniquity.

He nudged his horse forward. Gantry followed, still not entirely convinced.

A wide range of saloons, dance halls and theatres had been thrown up along the main street. In between, more normal premises catered for what one creative reporter called 'a floating population on a sea of alcohol'.

This so-called maritime population comprised all manner of human flotsam that had been washed up on the shores of Purgatory. Cowboys, nesters, renegade Indians, salesmen, Chinamen and trappers, to name but a few. Bottom of the heap came the Mexican peons. And way up there on top sat the road agents and gunmen who spent their ill-gotten gains in the dens of sin.

Red Meacher considered himself to be firmly at the top of the league.

He had spotted four such grandiose knights of the trail swaggering along the boardwalk. Thumbs hooked into tooled-leather gun-belts tied low on their hips, the strutting peacocks expected all and sundry to give way. Surly frowns told of dire retribution should any resistance be encountered.

One such unfortunate was not quick enough to step down into the muddy thoroughfare – a no-account greaser. A fist slammed into his jaw, spinning the poor wretch around. He yelped, falling into the mire, but made no attempt to retaliate. Then, like a whipped cur, he slunk away to lick his wounded pride.

Texas Red smiled. He had recognized the jasper who had thrown the punch. Laramie Nixx was a Montana rustler with whom Meacher had once contemplated joining forces. But the two were both leaders, not followers. Discretion soon led them to the conclusion that such a liaison would invariably lead to a confrontation. They had shaken hands in a Deadwood saloon, wished each other good fortune, and gone their separate ways.

This was the first time Meacher had run into his old buddy for three years. And he readily approved of Nixx's blunt tactics. This place was for him all right.

The pair drew rein outside a clapboard building, the largest on the street. There was no doubt in their minds that this was Pussy Cat Nell's place. A gaudy painting that depicted a giant yellow snake draped around the shoulder of a pretty gal was nailed above the entrance to the saloon.

Three drunken cowpoke's shouldered their way out of the door. Guns blazed into the air at a passing flock of meadowlarks. The squawking birds dispersed with none of them suffering a scratch. Such was the accuracy of the inebriated trio.

Meacher chuckled. The place hadn't changed one jot since his last visit. 'See what I mean, Lex? Believe me, we're gonna have us a whale of a time here.'

On entering the saloon, they were met by a solid wall of noise. A three-piece band was belting out a popular song over in one corner. Men were jigging around a dance floor, some with girls. Others lacking the wherewithal partnered each other. Everybody seemed to be heartily enjoying themselves.

Dominating the large room was the woman herself.

Nell Tucker was perched atop a stool on the balcony overseeing proceedings. This was no slinky feline purring contentedly. A large red bow fronted her blonde locks with glossy lipstick smeared across her warped features. The saloon boss was no oil painting and could have been any age between thirty and fifty. And she was clad in a voluminous yellow dress.

But Nell had presence. Her word was law, at least here in the Yellow Snake. Clutched in her hands was the famous shotgun. No doubt it was the same weapon that had despatched her foolish lover into the hereafter.

'Well, well, if'n it ain't Texas Red Meacher!' announced the woman in a loud grating voice. 'We've missed you. How long is it this time?'

The outlaw preened with delight as all eyes swung towards the two newcomers. He nudged his partner, relishing the attention. 'Must be over a year,' he called back, angling across to the bar where men moved aside to give these personages room. 'This is my partner, Lex Gantry. We sure are glad to be here.'

'Pleased to meet you, Lex. He sure is a handsome jasper, ain't he, girls?'

Immediately, a couple of feisty dames detached themselves from the bar and sauntered over, linking arms with the newcomers. Gantry's eyes popped at the amount of bare flesh on display. Perhaps Red had been right. It sure looked as if they were going to have a high old time here after all.

'The pleasure's gonna be all mine,' he replied.

'Got plenty of dough to spend I hope, boys,' Nell shot back. Money and its acquisition was never far from her thoughts.

'Enough.' Meacher was not about to divulge his haul to anybody, least of all a devious cat like Pussy Cat Nell. The pair had buried the saddle-bag and its contents some miles out of town by a cluster of rocks. No sense in placing temptation in anybody's way. They had sufficient funds about their persons to satisfy any immediate needs.

'You always were a careful dude, Tex,' Nell observed with a wry smirk.

'It pays to be.'

'Give the boys a couple of glasses, Charlie,' she ordered the chief bartender. 'As usual, the first bottle is on the house. Enjoy yourselves, boys.' Then she continued studying the rest of the room, humming along to the raucous melody.

Over the next few days, the pair of outlaws sampled most of the delights on offer. And there was no doubt that anything went in Purgatory. During that short period, three men had been shot in the street. Their crimes were diverse. One moonshiner had been caught watering down his liquor. A cheating gambler took umbrage when challenged and paid the ultimate price for his indiscretion.

Only the third victim was a member of the so-called elite.

Dooby Dan Keegan was piqued when one of his gang charmed away the woman he himself had taken a shine to. The result was a classic stand-off in the middle of the street watched by most of the town. Nell Tucker officiated at the duel giving the signal for the deadly contest to begin. Both men drew their irons together. Bullets flew, black powder smoke enveloping the scene of conflict.

Only when it had dispersed were the spectators able to see that Keegan had breathed his last. His rival, Idaho Jack, was now the leader of the infamous gang of road agents. He looked around, challenging anybody to take away his newly acquired crown. Nobody took up the gauntlet. And not a law officer in sight.

'This gang is gonna be called the Jackdaws,' he barked out, 'and I'm top bird. Everybody into the Yellow Snake. The drinks are on me.'

A cheer erupted, followed by a surge of rowdy humanity gravitating towards the saloon. Everybody loves a winner, especially a generous one.

Life was indeed cheap in Purgatory. Ever the cautious operator, Red Meacher knew when the writing was on the wall. Since his last sojourn in the town, the violence had escalated. And the outlaw had changed. He had become much more cynical, distrustful, acutely aware of his own mortality. Survival was the name of the game. And Red Meacher was not getting any younger.

Now that he had a substantial poke, he wanted to enjoy the good life. Continually fingering his six-shooter waiting for the next outburst of bloodshed was hard on the nerves. They were both having a good time, but with not even a Vigilance committee to administer some semblance of order, everybody took the law into their own hands.

All it might take was a wrong look, a mistaken nudge or a drunken argument over a girl and bullets could fly with no come back. That was the main reason why he decided it was much safer to head south for Mexico. Not to mention the fact that the senoritas were prettier, and the booze was cheaper down there.

Gantry readily agreed.

So the decision was made to pull out at the end of the week.

It was the day before the two outlaws planned to leave Purgatory that another pair of newcomers arrived in town. Heads lowered beneath their wide-brimmed straw sombreros, the two peasant labourers sat astride their donkeys. Their own horses had been left behind some rocks a few miles outside the town limits.

To all and sundry they gave the impression of dozing in the saddle. But appearances can be deceptive. Searching eyes panned the street eager to absorb the flavour of this wide-open berg referred to as the 'Sodom and Gomorrah of the Plains'.

Luther and Jay had decided to take the bull by the horns to determine whether their disguise held up. They were not disappointed. Nobody paid them any heed. Mexican peons were right at the bottom of the pecking order. Not worth a wooden dime.

Although the whole gamut of humanity was represented on the teeming main street, the female variety were in short supply. Only young women hurrying along to their jobs in the saloons and theatres were spotted. This was clearly a man's town and no place in which families could enjoy a peaceful life.

Jay was the first to see that they had come to the right place. He gestured to his partner. A casual finger pointed to the lone horse tied up outside the Yellow Snake. Etched on to the sorrel's rump was the distinctive 'LJ' brand of the La Junta livery stable.

'Well spotted, Jay,' muttered Luther under his breath. 'One of them must be inside. But where's the other jasper?'

They both quickly peered around. But, as far as they could judge, there was no sign of the second man. Not that these jiggers could be positively identified. All that was known about one of them was the distinctive colour of his hair. The other man had merely been described as 'gaunt-looking with a face coated in dark stubble' – a description that could easily fit half of the town's inhabitants.

The two men fixed each other with steely looks. They had indeed reached the culmination of their long ride. But what to do now? The next few minutes would determine whether it had been all worthwhile.

It was Luther who suggested that he should be the one to enter the saloon.

'Your ribs are still tender, and it's on account of me seeking retribution that we've come all this way.'

Jay tried remonstrating. 'Why don't we both go in? I can watch your back while you ask who owns the horse. Then we can lure him outside.'

But Luther was adamant. 'It would be best if'n you stayed here and kept a look out for the other dude. You'll know him by the LJ brand on his horse. Keep out of sight. If'n he shows before I'm finished with this one, you can deal with him as you think fit. We ain't taking no prisoners. It's them or us. Agreed?' Unknowingly, those prophetic words would come back to haunt him.

Jay's nod of concurrence was decisive.

'I'll try and keep the noise down with this.' Luther tapped the sheathed bowie knife hidden beneath the loose smock. 'But if'n you hear gunfire from in there, then come a-running.'

'Good luck, partner!' Jay murmured as they shook hands. Then Luther mounted the steps, momentarily pausing on the threshold of the saloon.

# CHAPTER FOURTEEN

# NEVER TRUST A SNAKE

Leaden feet prevented Luther from entering. It was not fear, nor even the fact that he had formed no viable plan of action. Thoughts were rushing through his head.

Would he be able to retrieve the hold-up money? Even then, could he secure the release of Skip Jenner and clear both their names? The alternative was a lengthy spell in jail – or a bullet from an outlaw's gun. Running was out of the question. Luther would not allow himself to abandon Skip to face the rigours of the law alone.

And what of Sally Manderson? Would she be waiting for him? He had left her so abruptly on that fateful day four weeks past with little explanation. And not even a goodbye kiss. His father had been murdered, which was reason enough in most people's eyes for a hurried departure, but would Sally understand?

Skip's new love, Lucy Barwise, had certainly given the young man her blessing. Would Sally have done the same?

A tight knot squeezed his guts testifying to the reality of the task he had set himself, and that it was about to reach its conclusion. There were no guarantees that it would play along his way. The last time he had felt like this was before the final charge led by General Grant at Petersburg.

All these thoughts flashed through his mind in the blink of an eye.

Then he pushed open the door and stepped inside. Adopting the cowed, brutalized shuffle of the subjugated peasant, he sidled over to the bar. It was crowded with a varied host of drinkers. All were pushing and shoving, calling out for the services of the three bartenders on duty.

While Luther waited his turn, he casually scanned the room.

His face was in shadow, hidden by the wide brim of the sombrero. There was no chance of the lone outlaw recognizing him. But equally, he could not have positively identified either of the men he was hunting. All he knew was that one had red hair, now short and far less conspicuous. There didn't appear to be anybody boasting the fiery head covering. That indicated that Meacher was absent.

But how to identify the other jasper quickly before

Meacher returned. This was the best time to act, while the enemy was divided – a standard military tactic.

Then an idea suddenly came into his head.

Over at the far end of the bar stood a rack of cubby holes with hooks on which door keys were hanging. They each had numbers between twenty-one and twenty-eight meaning they were on the second floor. A sign above read Luxury Rooms For Rent. The prices were exorbitant and likely to be occupied only by those in possession of the wherewithal. Red Meacher and his associate were definitely in that category.

It was, therefore, more than likely he had taken a room. The next poser was discovering which one. No use asking one of the barmen. Such enquiries from a simple peon would arouse instant suspicion . . . unless that peon was delivering an important message.

Lowering his head, Luther noticed some forms. They were for participants to sign up for a forthcoming horse race. Here was being presented a heaven-sent opportunity. He folded one of the forms up leaving it blank and wrote the name on the back: For Red Meacher – Personal and Private. Then he awaited his turn to get a drink.

A dime slid across the bar. '*Cerveza, por favor, señor.*'

Charlie Harrison looked down his beaky snout and sniffed. Peons were the lowest form of life, but money was money. He pushed the foaming glass of beer across the bar, spilling some of the contents on to Luther's smock. A warped smirk challenged this piece of garbage to retaliate. Luther smothered his anger with extreme difficulty. Then he handed over the note.

'This for Red Meacher . . . *es urgente.*' The barman's attitude changed abruptly. The name clearly meant something. Meacher must obviously be held in high esteem in the Yellow Snake. He took it and walked to the far end of the bar, placing the message in cubby hole number 26.

Luther concealed a smile. Now he had the room, but he needed to gain access. That key was the answer. The room must be locked and empty for it to be hanging there. Casually, Luther made his way over to the rack. Securing the key would be simple, provided nobody was looking in his direction.

Timing was crucial.

Nervous eyes panned the room. All three barmen were busy serving. Customers were intent on attracting their attention. Gamblers were avidly placing bets. It was now or never. A hand snaked out, grasped the key and slipped it into his pocket. There was no sudden outcry. Success was followed by a huge sigh of relief.

Levering himself off the bar, the bogus peon sidled towards the staircase. He slid under the overhang and quickly removed the disguise. A white-clothed figure wearing a sombrero would be instantly spotted mounting the stairs and challenged. One clad in regular range garb was more likely to be accepted as a patron on the upper floor.

With his head turned away from those in the bed of the saloon, Luther mounted the stairs. He was fortunate that Pussy Cat Nell was out of town checking on a new supplier of hard liquor.

His heart was firmly in his mouth until the empty

landing was reached and he was effectively out of sight. From there he hustled up to the top floor and quickly sought out Room 26. A quick knock followed to determine that the room was empty. With no response, he slid the key into the lock and quietly entered.

Now it was a question of hunting around to find the missing dough. Before conducting a search, he checked the window. His luck was still in. Outside was a useful veranda leading down to a back alley. A quick but thorough search revealed that the dough was not in the room. He cursed. So it must have been hidden somewhere safe. Meacher clearly didn't trust his fellow revellers in Purgatory.

So far everything had gone Luther's way. But this was a set-back. Maybe that was where the outlaw had gone. To replenish his funds. All of a sudden Luther had a problem. What to do now? The obvious choice was to hang around until one or other of them turned up.

Before he was afforded the chance to work out any proper strategy, the good fortune that had thus far helped him was abruptly terminated.

'What in thunder are you doing in here?' snarled an irate voice from the doorway.

The brusque demand for answers shattered the intruder's illusion of self-assurance. Luther abraided his folly. He had badly underestimated the enemy.

He had no way of knowing that the chief barman who had initially served Luther had been paid by Meacher to watch out for any suspicious characters. So when a dubious greaser had mentioned the outlaw by name, Charlie had kept him under covert surveillance.

All his movements had been surreptitiously followed.

So when Luther discarded the smock and went up the stairs, the bar snake immediately hurried across to inform Lex Gantry.

'You must be one of those pesky rats that have been chasing us. So where's the other skunk hiding?' Luther had his back to the speaker. He remained silent, desperately trying to figure a way out of this trap. 'Come on, out with it!' rapped Gantry. 'I ought to put a bullet in you right now. But Tex will be back soon. He can decide how best to deal with you. So let's make ourselves comfortable. Turn around slowly and drop your gun.'

Luther knew that once he discarded the Remington, he was helpless. His hand strayed to the water jug on the dresser beside which he was standing. As he turned, his hand was hidden from view. Quick as lightning he flung the pot at Gantry. The move took the outlaw by surprise, but he still managed to snap off a shot. The bullet blasted the jug into fragments. A second shot seared Luther's left arm. Nothing more than a flesh wound, but it still felt like a red hot poker.

Thankfully his shooting arm was untouched. Luther's own gun cleared leather and replied with three rapid fire shots. Only one hit the target. But it was a gut shot. The outlaw staggered back crashing into a mirror and tumbling to the floor.

That unholy racket was bound to have been heard two floors down. Only moments were left to find out where Meacher had stashed the dough before somebody arrived. A quick look at the outlaw's grey features was enough to show that his time was fast running out, along with his life blood.

'Where's the loot hidden, mister?' he pressed, urging the stricken man to confess. 'Your buddy is the last man standing. This is probably how he planned it all along.'

It was a throwaway line, but one that struck a chord with Lex Gantry. One by one his associates had been disposed of. Now it was his turn. His suspicions about Meacher's true intentions must have been right after all.

His fatally injured body was fast shutting down. And Lex knew it.

'There's a draw three miles north of town,' he gasped out, his chest heaving with the effort. 'Watch out for a rock shaped like an Injun's head at the entrance.' Luther nodded eagerly. He remembered commenting about the likeness to Jay. 'We buried the saddle-bag at the top end under a flat rock marked with a cross.'

The outlaw's eyes rolled up into his head. His face contorted in pain. But he was not ready to cash in his chips just yet. He struggled up, gripping the other man's arm. 'Watch out for Red scratching his left ear. That's when he'll make his play.'

The subtle warning was his final utterance. The blood-stained body arched in a convulsive shudder. Then he sank back with a deep sigh. Lex Gantry was dead.

And now there was only one.

On hearing the commotion inside the Yellow Snake,

Jay Barwise left his place of concealment in an alleyway and hustled over to the saloon. Drawing his gun from beneath the smock, he moved towards the door. But Jay was not the only interested spectator. Red Meacher had just returned from his trip to Indian Draw.

Anything could have initiated the gunfire inside the saloon. It was nothing new. It was the sudden appearance of a peon hurrying across the street, and toting a hog-leg that caught his eye. Unusual in itself, but there was something else about this particular greaser that was bugging the outlaw.

Then he remembered. It was the limp. This dude must be Barwise! Somehow the two critters had evaded Sad-Eye Villa's Comanche bucks. These guys seemed to lead charmed lives. Well, that was about to end.

The shooting inside the saloon had to be from his partner. Lex was in trouble. Meacher shrugged. Forget about him. But Barwise was here, and now at his mercy.

The outlaw crept up behind the hovering rancher. Jay had stopped to peer in through the grimy window trying to determine what was happening before he leapt into the fray. He never got the chance. A solidly placed gun barrel effectively shut out his lights.

Meacher caught the crumpling frame and heaved it over to Gantry's horse tethered close by. His old buddy would have to take his chances. Looking after number one was now the main priority. He hoisted the unconscious man on to the animal's back. Nobody paid him any attention. Just another peon getting what he deserved. It happened all the time.

Within moments of his arrival, he was heading back

the way he had come. A hand trailed behind leading the encumbered horse. Once he was safely back within the confines of Indian Draw, this dude was going to pay dearly for past afflictions perpetrated against what the crazed owlhooter judged was a maligned foe.

Meacher smiled. Catching this dude here in Purgatory was a stroke of luck. Now he had no need of returning to Wyoming. His nemesis had come to him.

And once the bastard had been dealt with, Texas Red would head south for Old Mexico. There was enough loot stashed away to last him a long time down there.

Meanwhile, back in the saloon, Luther knew that time was not on his side. Already, the pounding of heavy boots could be heard hustling up the stairs. In moments, seconds even, they would be here. He thrust up the sash window and clambered out on to the veranda. The backstairs were negotiated in record time. Stumbling on to his knees at the bottom, he ignored the jarring in his arm from the stray bullet.

A swing to the left and he was running up the alley. He drew to a halt behind a wagon and peered out on to the main street.

All eyes were focused on the ruckus emanating from the saloon. But of Jay Barwise, there was no sign. And Lex Gantry's horse had disappeared. Surely Jay would not have lit out and left him to the wolves.

Mingling with the growing crowd of onlookers, Luther gingerly enquired what was happening. One old trapper informed him that a hard-boiled tough named Lex Gantry had swapped lead with an intruder in his room.

'Darn it!' Luther exclaimed.

The startled oath caught the attention of the trapper. 'What's bugging you, mister?'

'Somebody has stolen my horse,' Luther ejaculated in mock irritation. 'It was tied up at yonder hitching rail.'

'I saw exactly what happened,' replied the old timer, eager to share his observations. 'Seems like some fella had a dispute with a greaser,' averred the trapper. 'He slugged the jasper, then threw him over your horse and rode off. Don't know what caused it, though.'

Luther bridled at the brazen effrontery. 'Damn hoss thief!' he snarled. 'Which way did they go?'

The trapper pointed to the northern end of town. But already his interest in the matter had faded. He moved away to obtain a better view of the burgeoning altercation inside the saloon. Luther lost himself in the crowd making sure to keep his head down.

Some of the patrons had emerged from the alley adjoining the saloon, the vigilant chief bartender among them. Guns drawn, searching eyes probed the milling throng. But picking out one man amidst the massed ranks was difficult. They soon gave up and went back inside. Nothing had been stolen. Sure a man had been killed. But that was nothing new in Purgatory.

Ensuring that nobody noticed, Luther led one of the donkeys down a side street opposite the Yellow Snake so that he could mount up unseen. All he had to do now was reach Indian Draw. Then he could decide how to rescue Jay, retrieve the hold-up money and deal with Red Meacher.

A roundabout route through a series of back lots and corrals eventually found him leaving the town. He joined the main trail a half mile beyond the Purgatory limits. But progress was slow.

Unlike a saddle horse, it was impossible to cajole the donkey into more than a gentle trot. The stubborn critter had a will of its own and frequently stopped altogether. Only by twisting its pointed ears was the rider able to coax it back into motion. Eventually, after much cussing and pummelling, he reached the place where the two men had hidden their horses. Both were still there.

It was mid-afternoon, therefore, before he finally approached the prominent rock where a side draw forked left. There was no knowing how far into the rocky fastness, the draw extended so he had to abandon the horses and continue on foot. It was initially unclear whether this side trail was well used. No evidence of shod hoof prints could be seen deviating from the main trail.

But Luther and his partner had been tricked like this once before. Moving along the draw, he came upon the evidence he sought after no more than fifty yards.

# CHAPTER FIFTEEN

# STAND-OFF

Another fifteen minutes of tentative walking brought him to a bend. Peeping round the side of a rock stack, he could see that this was where Indian Draw terminated.

And in the middle of a small amphitheatre was the camp-site of Texas Red Meacher. More important, however, was a grim sight that brought a lump to Luther's throat. Jay was staked out on the ground. His arms and legs were spread wide in the form of a cross. Meacher had a lump of iron heating in the fire. He took it out. The end glowed red hot.

And there was no doubt as to how he intended using the iron. The outlaw attempted a grin of triumph. It emerged more as a bestial twist, a warped scowl colder than a mountain stream.

'I've waited a long time for this moment,' he snarled out. A brutal kick urged the woozy captive out of the empty void. 'You hear me, Sergeant "Whipcrack" Barwise? Now it's payback time. Eight years on – and I can still feel the searing cut of that hide on my back.'

Another kick ensured that Jay was fully conversant with his captor's intentions. The red hot poker wafted before his eyes. Fear registered on the victim's ashen features. He tried pulling away, but there was nowhere to run. An ugly smirk assured the recipient that no mercy would be forthcoming.

Meacher was enjoying himself. He intended to savour his revenge to the full.

The poker came closer, the heat of its glowing tip singeing Jay's eyebrows. Much as he tried to remain stoic in the face if this gruesome torture, a croak of terror issued from between gritted teeth.

A manic howl of delight gushed from the sadistic tormentor as the glowing iron was removed and put back into the hot embers. Meacher wanted his victim to suffer agonies of the mind before the physical torture was applied. 'Shout all you want, sucker,' he cackled rocking gleefully on his haunches. 'Nobody's gonna hear you stuck out in this wilderness.'

'Why don't you just shoot me and be damned?' Jay gasped out.

'That would be too easy, mister,' snapped the outlaw. 'I want you to suffer like you made me suffer all those years ago.'

The puzzled frown told Meacher that this guy had forgotten. Private Red Meacher – Prisoner 2986 . . . just another piece of stockade trash who had been tickled with that darned bull whip. 'You don't even have the shame to remember, do you, Sergeant?' Black eyes drilled into the starring face of his old enemy. 'March of '65? The POW stockade at Levenworth? I can still hear the crack of that whip. Now do you recall?'

Jay's face assumed a grim snarl of disdain. He nodded, remembering all too well. This was the skunk who had sliced up his brother from ear to ear.

'You deserved every stroke of that lash for killing my brother.' He tried to raise himself but the bonds held him down. 'Sure, Frank was a wayward kid, but he didn't deserve to have his throat ripped open down some back alley.'

'He was cheating at cards,' rasped the outlaw. 'Nobody makes a fool of Texas Red Meacher.'

Jay snorted out his contempt for the man standing over him now. 'You're lying. You were the cardsharp. And you just couldn't abide a better player winning.'

His eyes blazed with impotent fury. Here was the skunk who had killed his brother, yet he was the one going to die. But Jay Barwise was not about to give this rat the satisfaction of begging for mercy.

'Think yourself lucky you escaped with a flogging,' he snarled. 'The tribunal wanted you strung up on the gallows. But the War was almost over. I persuaded them to curtail your sentence because you were drunk. That was my biggest mistake. In return they insisted that a message had to be sent out to others of your kind. As the guy in charge it was my duty to carry out that punishment.'

'And you enjoyed applying every last stripe, didn't you?' Meacher had shut his mind to his own shortcomings in the incident. His burning soul was afire with the need to assuage a bitter hatred that had festered and grown over the years. He launched another boot at the tethered body.

Jay stifled a yell of pain as he felt his ribs cave in. The crack was audible.

'Enough of this jawing,' declared Meacher. 'It's show-time, buddy. And you are top of the bill. Prepare to receive the Meacher brand on your miserable hide.'

He walked over to the fire and removed the iron, now glowing white hot.

Hidden behind the stack overlooking the deadly scene of torment, Luther knew that he had to do something without delay. His partner's life now hung in the balance. A hand reached for the trusty Remington. Although he could not hear what was being said, the outlaw's attempt to inflict mental anguish on to his victim was almost palpable. And it enabled Luther to move closer. All of Red Meacher's attention was fastened on to his victim.

But now it was clear that his patience had run out. He hovered over his victim like a predatory eagle, the glowing iron ready to plunge.

Luther moved out into the open behind the menacing presence. 'Lay that iron down, mister, or I'll drill you where you stand.' The challenge was completely unexpected. Meacher froze on the spot, the branding iron held aloft. 'I said "Drop it",' Luther rapped out. 'You won't get another chance. My trigger finger is itching.'

'The only place this iron is going is down on to your friend.' Meacher's reply was measured and calm yet full of menace. 'Kill me now and I'll fall with it right on to him. Do you want that on your conscience?'

The iron was directly above the supine figure. Luther hesitated, suddenly thrown back on to the defensive. He cursed his folly, knowing the rat had him stymied. He had left it too late before making his play.

Now it was a fully fledged Mexican stand-off.

'So what happens now?' snarled Luther.

'I'll make you a deal.' Meacher said, not moving a muscle. 'Holster that gun and we can do this properly. Man to man. Winner takes all.'

Silence enfolded the draw as Luther considered his options. Shoot the guy down and he would place Jay's life in serious peril.

Accept the killer's taunting challenge and his own life would be on the line. Luther was no hard-assed gunslinger, unlike this jasper who lived by the gun. Could he match him and come out on top? Both his and Jay's lives were now at stake. There was only one course of action he could take.

Then he recalled Lex Gantry's last crucial piece of advice.

'I accept,' he called out. 'Turn around slow and easy. I'll leather my gun while you discard the iron. Then we'll see who is the faster.'

Meacher smiled. 'North versus South all over again. But this time the result will be different.'

As if in slow motion the two men swung to face each other. Luther hooked out his father's pocket watch. The fine Hunter had been presented by the citizens of Rawhide in California after Hardcap Sam Pickett cleaned up their town by getting rid of all the riff-raff. He gingerly flicked open the lid and placed it on the ground.

A lilting cadence immediately filled the hollow. Mellifluous and soothing, its melodic chime was in stark contrast to the lethal game of chance being enacted.

'When the music stops, make your play, and not before. Agreed?'

Meacher nodded, his warped features cracking into a sidewinder's noxious smile. A half minute passed before the tempo began to slow. The two men tensed, hunkering down ready for the showdown. Meacher lifted his hand to scratch his left ear just before the final notes waned. At the same time the outlaw was clawing for his hog-leg.

Luther threw himself to one side. He should have expected nothing less from this poisonous braggart. Gantry's warning was a godsend.

A bullet from Meacher's gun parted his hair as his own weapon barked. The outlaw staggered back as the slug grazed his temple. The gun fell from his hand. Quickly recovering, he bent down and grabbed hold of the branding iron lifting it to stab down on to the pinioned captive.

Again Luther's gun spat lead taking the outlaw in the chest. He didn't stop until the gun clicked on empty. With each hit, Meacher tottered backwards under the lethal salvo finally tumbling on to the searing iron. A spine-chilling howl of agony could not suppress the awful sizzle of burning flesh.

The outlaw's body twitched and bucked, his face contorting into a mask of unspeakable torment. Luther walked over and despatched the suffering villain as if he were no more than a lame horse. He took no pleasure in the deadly act. An eye for eye. The slate was now clean.

Once again silence descended over Indian Draw, now a field of death.

He hurried over to release Jay. The two men gasped and wretched, barely able to concede that their quest was finally over. No words could convey the starkly brutal reality of their ordeal as each relived his brush with the Grim Reaper.

But now it truly was over. Luther had avenged his father's murder. The hold-up money had been recovered – at least most of it. And they had the body of the red-headed outlaw to prove the innocence of both Luther and Skip Jenner.

With Texas Red Meacher strapped over the saddle of the donkey, his two pursuers headed back north, eager to rid themselves of No Man's Land and its lawless reputation. Neither of them would ever forget the Long Ride to Purgatory.

Luther hoped that in his case, the love of a good women would help erase the smell of death that now suffused his whole being.

# AUTHOR'S NOTE

The rectangular strip of land known as the Oklahoma Panhandle got its name in 1907 after statehood was granted. It first came into being after the independent state of Texas was accepted into the Union in 1845. A condition under the ordnance known as the Missouri Compromise stipulated that the land area of the new Texas (Tejas under Mexican rule) was too large. A section needed to be discarded to comply with a Slave State–Free State balance.

And thus the Panhandle came into being. Before that it was generally referred to as No Man's Land. Sandwiched between four territories, it fell under the jurisdiction of none. It was bounded by Kansas/Colorado and Texas to the north and south respectively, with New Mexico and Indian Territory (later Oklahoma) to west and east. A tiny area only 170 miles long by 34 miles wide compared to the vastly expanded United States of America, this anomalous tract achieved a reputation far in excess of its diminutive size.

Here was the perfect opportunity for all manner of skulduggery to thrive with no fear of retribution from the official authorities.

The name of Purgatory is a figment of the author's imagination. Not so White City, which was an actual place named due to the proliferation of tents. Those were soon replaced by more permanent structures. The name of Beer City was suggested due to an equal preponderance of saloons. The foaming brew was brought down the Santa Fe Trail from Dodge City north of the border in Kansas.

Hard liquor served in the saloons was a head-splitting potato moonshine provided by local sodbusters. Pussy Cat Nell has also gone down in history as the owner of the Yellow Snake Saloon. Here she applied her own form of frontier justice, of which Lew Bush suffered the consequences for his clandestine behaviour.

The rest makes for an exciting tale, much of which might well have taken place in this lawless territory.